Published by Rossendal

11 MowgrainView, Bacup,
Rossendale, Lancashire
OL13 8EJ
England

Published in paperback 2009

© Copyright Robert Sutton 2009

ISBN   978-1-906801-17-5

LIBERTIES, RIGHTS AND NON-RIGHTS

A Short Critique

By

R. H. Sutton

RB

Contents

Introduction

This book is about *rights*. It is not, however, a survey of human rights practice or malpractice; there are other books on rights abuses as under Nazism, the Stalinist purges, the activities of Pol Pot, etc. Likewise, there are more specialized books dealing exclusively with women's rights, ethnic rights, minority rights and so on. Rather differently, the purpose of this book is to clarify what exactly a right *is*.

Most people are perfectly well aware that freedom and anarchy, for example, are very different things. On the other hand the definition of freedom turns out to be surprisingly intricate. Philosophers, rights theorists and legal theorists make useful and informative distinctions between liberties, freedoms, permissions, claims, prerogatives and so on. Rights subdivide, therefore, into different *types* of rights.

But in ordinary parlance they are all called 'rights' which can sometimes lead to vagueness and ambiguity. Certain puzzles need to be unravelled too, for example is it possible to be 'within your rights' but also 'in the wrong' over something? More broadly, another question is to distinguish between laws or declarations about rights and the principles upon which the laws or declarations are based. What are those principles, and how do we justify them?

It is virtually a commonplace to say that all human beings have rights, as obvious, almost, as saying that all human beings have bodies, or minds. But generalities tend to disguise complexity. That is why we take an analytical approach to rights in which we seek to clarify not only what rights are, but also what they are not. Likewise, although a small number of rights are clear and unequivocal, many others are more relative and uncertain.

One - Rights, Non-Rights and Responsibilities

When is a right not a right?   This is not a trick
question; it relates to perfectly real issues, both
major and minor.   Jason believes he has a right to
play loud music all day long but his neighbours
have other ideas.   Who is right about their rights
and who is wrong?   They can't both be right - or if
so, how, exactly?   What if people are mistaken on
the rights they think they have?   One thing is
certain - there is frequent disagreement and conflict
on rights, over all sorts of issues.

Your right to speak your mind could infringe
another person's right not to be offended or insulted
if you are not careful.   The railwaymen claim a
right to go on strike, but commuters have rights to
go to work.   The freedom of the press will be
defended on the grounds of 'the public's right to
know' about this, that or the other but it will be
criticized by people concerned about press invasion
of the right to privacy.   Some women regard
abortion as a woman's *right*, but others regard
abortion as wrong.

Rights can also be very complex and subtle, for
example the right to equality.   In the UK we have
the right to equality before the law, but this does not
mean that every accused person should be found
equally innocent.   What, precisely, does equality
mean in this context?   Or again, if your job is more
complex, responsible and demanding than another
less onerous job, most people would agree that you
should have a right to be paid more.   So there can
be rights to pay differentials for valid reasons,

giving rights to *inequality*. What, then, do equality rights mean?

It is commonly believed that rights are 'fundamental'. It is often assumed that if something is contrary to your rights it is an infringement or a violation of your rights and therefore *wrong*, but this is not necessarily so. For example denial of freedom rights can be necessary even in the most liberal societies when violent and dangerous individuals have to be locked up to protect the safety rights of others. The laws against slander are a partial denial of my right to free speech, but there are very good reasons for those laws - in particular, that neither I nor anyone else should say false things about you. Clearly it is sometimes right to deny rights. Denial of rights is not necessarily a wrong, and we can give plenty of other examples. Joe Soap has a right to believe, if he wants to, that the world is flat, but if he is a teacher he has no right to promulgate beliefs for which there is ample evidence to the contrary. There can be *non-rights* as well as *rights*.

It is often more appropriate to talk of *limitations, curtailments* or *setting boundaries* to rights rather than 'denials'. But it is equally important to distinguish between limitations, curtailments etc. for *valid* reasons and for *invalid* reasons. In the UK the laws against slander are not an invalid infringement of free speech for the reason we have just outlined, whereas the laws against political dissent in the Soviet Union *were* an infringement of free speech, suppressing open debate and valid criticism.

The right to life is often said to be absolute and should not have limits or boundaries of any sort, but even here there can be differences of view. Plenty of people believe in the validity of abortion for non-medical reasons, capital punishment, soldiers killing in the defence of their own country, or killing in self-defence if you are attacked and your life is in peril. We shall look at some of these issues later on.

It is true to say that for any assertion of a right, we can always reasonably ask 'but should that *be* a right?'. I might say that free speech is a fundamental right but another person might ask 'why?' or she might say 'maybe it's fundamental but it's certainly not absolute'. We then discuss the ethics of speaking freely and I note that whether I have a right to free speech or not, it is *wrong* to tell lies, to exaggerate, to slander or libel other people, to incite to race hatred, to insult or offend people gratuitously or to shout 'fire!' in a crowded theatre without due cause. These considerations are also 'fundamental'. Rights can always be questioned, appraised, confirmed, limited, qualified or denied in terms of what is good or bad, fair or unfair, or similar ethical criteria. Rights can also be assessed, incidentally, as consistent or inconsistent, practical or impractical, sensible or silly, and so on.

The most important point is that rights and responsibility go together. I have a right to free speech which I must exercise *responsibly*. This is a responsibility towards others, but with many other sorts of rights I can also have responsibilities towards *myself*. For example I have rights that other people should not be culpably negligent of my personal safety, but I also have responsibilities for my own safety and I cannot always blame other people for genuine accidents or my own carelessness.

The main exceptions where there can be rights without responsibilities would be babies, infants, the comatose, the insane etc.   Otherwise, if you neglect your responsibilities you can be open to criticism.   If you cause harm to others you will *forfeit* your rights, or some of them.   You can be *liable*, and it is naive to misperceive 'having rights' as exonerating you in some way.   For human beings to regard themselves primarily as rights-holders with no concept of responsibility towards others (or towards themselves) is a misconception at best and dangerous at worst.   *Rights dogmatism* tends to gloss over these issues.   And what if the selfish, the immature and the manipulative over-emphasize rights for self-seeking ends?

Rightly or wrongly, many people now perceive rights as *problems*.   It is not always clear whether rights are the problem or the people who have them, but all the same, rights are perceived as dysfunctional if serious problems such as crime are not properly addressed through placing too much emphasis on the rights of the anti-social.   What if a streetwise delinquent despises the law because 'they can't hurt me because I've got my rights'?   Unruly children seem to be beyond discipline because of their rights; the criminal justice system seems to be more concerned with the rights of the criminal than with victims' rights, and so on.   Rights 'tunnel-vision' and political correctness (which go hand-in-hand) seem to be the dominant ethos in the media, law, government, social work and in many professions.

It is a truism that human rights are 'fundamental' in the sense that they are very *important*, to everyone. Human rights are necessary conditions for valid human objectives to be realized and for valid interests to be protected. But other things are equally fundamental such as *obligation*, *responsibility* and *accountability*, without which there would be no such things as rights at all. Rights are part of a broader whole. Also, many rights can be limited, curtailed or forfeited for perfectly valid reasons, and many are conditional. We are told that rights are 'fundamental', 'absolute', 'immutable', 'basic', 'inherent', 'inalienable' and so on, but other than rhetoric what precisely do these words mean?

It is equally important to ask what they do not mean, or should not mean. Personal liberty and freedom cannot be absolute or unconditional otherwise they would conflict with *other people's* rights which may be more important. 'Freedom' does not entitle you to kill or steal just as you like because other people have rights *not* to be robbed or killed. And in everyday life your spouse, your children and many other people may have valid claims on your time which you are not always 'at liberty' to ignore.

The idea of inalienable rights leads to the view that rights should never be rescinded by anyone other than the rights-holder. This is true with certain 'prerogative rights' (see also Chapter Four), for example under normal circumstances nobody other than yourself has the right to release someone from a promise they have made to you. Presumably too, in countries where euthanasia is legal, you and only you can validly sign a document rescinding your own right to life.

But many other rights can be validly rescinded by other people because they are *forfeitable*. If society rescinds the freedom rights of violent and dangerous criminals and sends them to prison, this is for compelling and overriding reasons which are not at the discretion of the rights-holders. Your right to keep your job is very important, but if you are repeatedly absent from work without good reason you might lose your job if you are not careful. If you have forfeited your own rights it makes no sense to say that someone else has infringed them. Rights can also be lost through *force of circumstances* which, again, are not always the same as *infringement*. If your employer has to close down for reasons beyond his control, it is difficult to impute blame against him (but see also Chapter Three on compensatory rights such as redundancy pay).

Theorists on rights make a number of important distinctions between different *types* of rights which we shall explain and elaborate as this book progresses. For example we can distinguish between 'negative' and 'positive' rights. Negative rights are that certain things should *not* be done by other people, including your rights *not* to be lied to, defrauded, robbed, attacked, raped, tortured, murdered, enslaved, persecuted or discriminated against. These particular examples are among the most important rights and are arguably 'absolute'. Positive rights are that certain things *should* be done by other people, e.g. to tell you the truth, keep a promise, repay a debt, etc. These rights too are very important ones. But positive rights also include 'substantive' rights to specific goods, services, benefits etc. which, as we shall see, can sometimes be *contingent* upon other people's abilities or inabilities to provide them. Such rights can therefore be *uncertain*, without necessarily implying *default* or *infringement* by others.

The most perplexing issues concern conflicts of rights, which often result in compromises being made. How can there be compromise, though, if rights are supposedly 'fundamental'? It is desirable to avoid conundrums such as 'can there be occasions when a fundamental right is only semi-fundamental?' or 'can an absolute human right sometimes be only partly absolute instead of absolutely absolute?' Many questions are discussed in terms of rights, but this is prone to introduce a polarization of issues that are more complex than rights just in themselves.

At the end of this chapter we shall look at a detailed example of how different rights can conflict and how one right can validly override another one. Prior to that we shall look at what exactly a right *is*, but firstly we must dispose of various misconceptions about rights which tend to produce muddled thinking. For example there are certain vague generalizations about rights which are often quoted as basic principles but which really say very little. Sentences such as 'all human beings have rights' or 'people have rights because they are human beings' are, from a semantic point of view, *platitudes*.   Like tautologies, such sentences are 'true' but essentially uninformative, and do not in themselves entail particular conclusions that we have specific rights to *this* or to *that*.   In Chapter Two we shall see how rights, claims for rights and laws about rights have a clearer basis on *ethical* grounds which will be more precise than platitudes or clichés.

We must also avoid the misleading notion of having 'natural' or 'inherent' rights as if they are 'part of what we are'.   We do not 'have rights' in the same literal way as we have *attributes* such as bodies or minds.   Rights are about freedoms, claims and entitlements arising out of the personal, social, moral, legal and political *relationships* between human beings; as such, rights are *relational* concepts, they are not intangible *things* which we walk around with.   'My rights' are real enough, but they are not, literally speaking, 'part of what I am'.   This is purely metaphorical.

Another misconception, which we shall return to in Chapter Three, is to equate rights with needs, interests, aspirations and so on.   Rights are often *about* needs, interests etc., in many cases quite important ones, but this is not the same as saying that needs and rights are identical or that the one entails the other.   As a matter of pure logic (quite apart from anything else) the sentence 'I need a drink' does not entail 'I have a right to a drink', and the same applies to any other line of reasoning of that format unless further explanation is given. Philosophers call this the 'naturalistic fallacy', of which the doctrine of 'natural rights' is a prime example.

So - what is a right? The major distinction made by most theorists is between *liberty rights* and *claim-rights*. A *liberty* arises if an action is neither compulsory nor prohibited. If you have no *duty not* to do something, then you may do it or not do it, as you wish. It is an *option*. For example if there are no laws or other constraints against travelling from A to B, then you are 'at liberty' to do so. But that is all it means, and this is a very precise definition. Liberties do not entail *obligations* by others, e.g. to take you there or provide a bus service. Liberties are unrelated to obligations by others, whilst *freedom*, as we shall see, is different.

Claim-rights differ quite markedly from liberties and are *based upon* specific obligations by others, e.g. a promise to be kept, your salary to be paid, a benefit to be provided, the truth to be told, lies not to be told, etc.. A claim-right is defined by its correlation with obligations towards you on the part of other people. For example your right to be told the truth correlates with the obligation of others to be truthful. That is what defines your right to be told the truth. Your freedom (see also Chapter Four) correlates with the obligations of others not to interfere with you, subject to one or two provisos. If you have a right not to be violently attacked then, if this means anything at all, it means that other people have an obligation not to violently attack you - otherwise, what else does it mean? To say that other people are obliged not to attack you and that you have a right not to be attacked are really two ways of saying the same thing.   In Chapter Two we shall look at the basis of *obligation.*

This analysis distinguishes a *right* from simply a want, a need, a wish or a desire.   It also strengthens the idea of a right.   If your rights are based upon other people's obligations you have a firm basis for holding them accountable if they neglect or infringe your rights.   You can look them in the eye and remind them of their obligations, something you can 'get a handle on' which is much clearer than woolly notions of natural rights which are 'part of what we are'.   This is both the strength and the weakness of rights.   If a right correlates with a clearly identifiable obligation by others then it has *leverage.*   But if a right you seek, or think you have, cannot be correlated with an obligation by others, then it is not a right after all.   Some obligations by others can be very clear and unequivocal, whilst others can be more contingent and uncertain, or even non-existent.

Also, rights do not mean that you go around inventing obligations by others willy-nilly.   It is important to avoid a 'shopping list' perception of rights as a set of claims or demands which take no account of the rights of others.   What would *your* reaction be if you are suddenly faced with a set of new obligations you never knew you had?   Many well-meaning   individuals   and   organizations proclaim that people should have rights to this, that or the other, but who picks up the tab?   In many cases one person's rights are another person's liabilities, but they have rights too.   This is an awkward little detail which some people (who often have a lot to say about rights) tend to 'gloss over', or not notice at all.   But what if this results in rights imbalance?

For example, consider employment law in the UK. Governments have steadily passed legislation over the years which has enhanced the rights of employees, much of which has been good and necessary. Few would wish to go back to the bad old days when you could be made redundant without a pennyworth of compensation, and few would wish to reinstate the days when a black person could be refused employment because he was black, or a woman passed over for promotion purely because she was a woman.

But more recently laws have been passed which have begun to affect the rights of employers.   If employers are faced with an ever-increasing list of statutory requirements to provide employees with leave of absence for an ever-increasing list of reasons, who bears the cost and the inconvenience? 'Substantive' rights (to benefits, goods, services etc.) *always* entail obligations by others, but too many rights only produces 'obligation overload' on other people.   In most cases employers are fair-minded people who recognize employees' needs for maternity leave etc., but do employers receive adequate recompense for losses incurred from the state which initiated the legislation?

Now consider a very different issue.   Most human beings are normally responsible for their own actions, but what about a paranoid schizophrenic who genuinely cannot help his own actions?   If he has not killed or hurt anyone (*yet*), can it be right to deprive him of liberty?   To most people the answer is perfectly clear: society should have the right to curtail his freedom rights pre-emptively, on public safety grounds, specifically the rights of *others* not to be attacked or killed. Obviously a paranoid schizophrenic cannot help being a paranoid schizophrenic and he is not culpable in a moral sense. But that is not the point. The point is that he is still a serious danger to others, and it was reported in 2007 that on average one person per week is killed in the UK by the mentally ill. It is pertinent to ask what is going on, or not going on.

One answer is that governments, legislators and other relevant parties have to be perfectly clear as to which rights should have priority - one person's freedom rights or another person's rights not to be attacked or killed? If, behind it all, we have a perception of rights where all rights are *equally fundamental*, then we have in theory a permanent *impasse* between a schizophrenic's right to civil liberties and other people's rights not to be attacked or killed. This identifies the *rights deadlock* problem which human rights fundamentalism often seems to overlook. But on many issues some rights *have to* override others, otherwise the concept of a right is incoherent. Legislation which merely lists rights but fails to clarify which types of rights should take precedence over others may therefore be prone to *ad hoc* interpretation and inconsistency, leaving to chance the rights of ordinary citizens to personal safety and to 'go about their lawful business without let or hindrance'.

So, by what principles should one right override another one? One of the most frequently quoted but least helpful pronouncements on rights is probably philosopher Ronald Dworkin's assertion that 'rights are trumps' (*Taking Rights Seriously*, 1977). This means that the rights of the *individual* should always 'trump' the actions of governments purporting to represent the common good. This is clearly relevant in certain contexts, but not in all. For if the government is democratically elected and represents the legitimate rights of the majority of the people, the rights of 'the individual' may conflict not with the government *as such* but with the rights of other people *who are also individuals*. We therefore have a dilemma - whose rights trump whose? Just as it stands, Dworkin's 'rights are trumps' argument merely takes us round in circles from one person's rights to another's like a never-ending merry-go-round.

It all depends on *which* rights you are talking about and the *criteria* for one right to take precedence over another. Thus, if society rescinds the freedom rights of dangerous criminals and sends them to prison, or looks after paranoid schizophrenics in secure institutions instead of 'care in the community', other people's rights not to be killed or attacked are normally considered to be *overriding*. Loss of life or serious injury is a *greater harm* than loss of liberty, giving a valid reason for one right to override another one. The criterion, therefore, is the *comparative harm* principle and it is important that human rights legislation makes this sufficiently clear. We shall look at this principle more closely in the next chapter.

Rights are said to be inalienable and immutable, but unless these terms are purely rhetorical we would suggest that a right is inalienable or immutable *if and only if* it cannot be *validly* overridden by any other rights, duties or actions of others.   But only a small number of rights fall into this category, i.e. those rights which should never be altered, ignored or denied under any circumstances for example your right not to be unwarrantably killed.   It is important to distinguish these from many other rights which can be varied, lost or forfeited for valid reasons.   The classic example is your right to personal liberty if you are a danger to others for whatever reason.   *Few* rights are 'absolute'; most rights vary in importance from one to another according to circumstances and many other considerations.

Two - Basic Principles

It is useful to take a bird's eye view of rights in general terms. In the UK, we have rights to free speech, to freedom, to life, liberty, education, to freedom of association, to freedom from coercion, to travel, to equality before the law, to vote in elections, to go about one's lawful business without let or hindrance, to purchase or sell property, to trade, to free health care at the point of delivery, to legal defence and counsel if you are on trial in a court of law, to free schooling, to an old age pension, to social security if you are out of work, and many other rights. Certain rights are formulated negatively, e.g. the rights *not* to be robbed, attacked, raped or murdered, the rights *not* to be discriminated against in respect of race, creed or gender, or the right *not* to be unfairly dismissed from your employment. Many rights are specified and reflected in laws, and some countries incorporate rights in written constitutions.

Of course, some rights are *conditional*. Only people who are medically qualified have the right to practise as doctors. Only people who meet the requisite criteria have a right to Income Support. Often, rights may be based on a person's position in a hierarchy or on their role in society. Variations in rights can be fair or unfair, reasonable or unreasonable as the case may be. But certain other sorts of rights are held to be more basic, having nothing to do with your position or role in society, for example your right to free speech or your rights not to be deceived, robbed and so on.

Many rights are *political* in character, e.g. the right to vote in elections, stand for Parliament, etc.. Others are *legal* in character, e.g. the right to appeal if you are found guilty of something, and so on. There are *religious* rights, most notably the right of freedom of worship.   There are *economic* rights such as the right to engage in trade.   Rights of *benefit* include education, health care, old age pensions etc..   There are *contractual* rights, e.g. to be paid the wage or salary that is specified in your contract of employment.   There are *moral* rights, such as the rights to life, liberty, respect, personal privacy, the right to be told the truth, and so on.

It is very important to distinguish between *legal rights* and *moral rights*.   They often coincide, for example the laws against theft constitute your legal right not to be robbed, but there is also a moral right not to be robbed.   Further, legal rights as such only exist insofar as the relevant laws exist.   They do not exist if the laws do not exist, before they have become laws or after the laws have been repealed or amended.   Moral rights by contrast are held to exist irrespective of whether there are laws about them or not.   Thus black South Africans in the apartheid era had no legal rights or only the most rudimentary ones, but they still had *moral* rights which were seriously abused.   And the same applied, 'perfectly legally', to the Jews in Nazi Germany and to the kulaks in the Soviet Union in the 1930's.

In terms of the standard human rights 'credo', all human beings in all human societies are said to have 'basic human rights'.   These include the rights to life, liberty, equality, to free speech, to respect, to justice and to many other things. We all have rights irrespective of race, gender, age, circumstances, position or role in society or who we are. Likewise the same rights apply to all human beings irrespective of cultural belief systems, laws or the policies or ideologies of governments. Rights are said to be 'immutable' and 'inalienable', meaning that if they are varied, taken away or denied this constitutes an infringement or an abuse of rights. We have already encountered (and criticized) some of these ideas, but all of them are confidently proclaimed to be 'self-evidently' and fundamentally true.

These ideas are to be found within the 1948 Universal Declaration of Human Rights by the United Nations which includes, interestingly, *substantive* rights to food, clothing, medical care, to shelter and to various other material benefits. We say 'interestingly' because the Declaration fails to specify *who*, exactly, has the obligation to provide these benefits or with what resources. Because of this, there can be differences of view as to whether these are really rights or not (more on this later).

Not many people realize that in historical terms, human rights ideas (and rights terminology) are comparatively recent. In ancient times Plato and Aristotle wrote about politics and justice but not about human rights *as such*. Likewise you will not find human rights or natural rights mentioned as such in the Christian Bible although it did, of course, have a lot to say about what is good or bad, right or wrong.

Rights first appeared as a political and a legal concept in the Middle Ages as in Magna Carta in 1215 and in the writings of various theorists. 'Rights' in its modern form developed further in the seventeenth and eighteenth centuries when Western philosophers began to develop theories of 'social contracts' and 'natural rights'. Not long afterwards, the American Declaration of Independence, 1776, and the French Revolution in 1789 both placed special emphasis on rights. The American Declaration of Independence asserted that 'all men.....are endowed by their Creator with certain inalienable rights.... Life, Liberty and the pursuit of Happiness...'; the French Revolution proclaimed *liberté, égalité, fraternité* - and so on.

In many ways the modern idea of 'human rights' is basically a reiteration of 'natural rights'. The conceptual issues and problems are much the same in either case, and we have already discussed some of these in Chapter One. For 'rights' as a doctrine has been controversial almost from the start. Edmund Burke (1729-1797) criticized natural rights in *Reflections on the Revolution in France* (1790). The philosopher Jeremy Bentham (1748-1832) criticized natural rights as 'nonsense on stilts', 'dangerous nonsense', and Karl Marx (1818-1883) also criticized rights. Further criticism has continued in more recent times. In *Rights Talk – The Impoverishment of Political Discourse* (1991) by Mary Ann Glendon the social and political dangers of over-emphasizing rights are made very clear. What if too much 'rights talk' ignores *responsibility* and only exacerbates conflict rather than resolving it?

Human rights are incorporated into the laws, legal systems and constitutions of many countries, but this does not in itself give them *veracity*. We may be told that *this* or *that* is a fundamental human right because 'it says so' in *this* law or *that* declaration, but this is taking things for granted. Beliefs and ideas, about rights or anything else, are not validated simply because they are written down in the laws or declarations which uphold or enforce them. They can still be flawed, or even fallacious.

What we need to get at are the principles that lie behind the words written on the pieces of paper, but it is circular to seek answers by appealing to the laws or the declarations themselves. Also, apart from tautologies there are very few 'self-evident truths' about anything at all. We could perhaps regard human rights beliefs as basically a set of ideals, but here again there are difficulties. We can *choose* our ideals, so they can mean anything we like. This is hardly a viable basis for a set of principles which are supposed to be binding upon everyone.

This brings us to *ethics*. However, rights and ethics are often believed to be different and separate. Many people believe that rights are fundamental, basic etc. etc. but that ethics and morality are subjective and relative, i.e. matters of personal value belief, culture, 'lifestyle choice' or simply preference. But this view is implicitly self-contradictory for it is often overlooked that rights are based upon ethics in the first place. Read, for example, the Universal Declaration on Human Rights. Even if we don't agree with everything it says, what is it other than a set of moral imperatives about how people should or should not behave towards each other?   Or if your rights are infringed or rescinded without due cause, you will probably complain that is wrong or unfair.   But 'wrong' and 'unfair' are ethical concepts so again, it is not so easy to say that rights and ethics are separate from each other.   And if ethics are relative then so, necessarily, are rights, and if *that* is true then how can they be 'basic', 'fundamental', and so on?

There is a popular but fallacious view that when we make moral statements (such as 'it is right to tell the truth', 'it is wrong to offend other people' etc.) we are only expressing our own personal attitudes or feelings about things.   But this overlooks a very pertinent question - why do we use *adjectives* such as 'good', 'bad', 'right', 'wrong' which we apply to actions, events, people and so on?   We do not just go around saying 'I approve of *this*' or 'I don't like *that*'.   If Julia says 'dishonesty is wrong' she is saying something about *dishonesty*, not about *herself* - and if she is asked *why* it is wrong she does not say 'because it's a feeling I've got' or 'I don't like it'.   Most people know the difference between saying something is *wrong* as against 'feeling talk' such as 'unacceptable', 'objectionable' etc. etc..   Again, not all senses of 'good' are about expressing feelings, attitudes or approval.   Suppose we want to say something much stronger than 'I approve of respecting others', for example - suppose we want to say 'it is *necessary* that we respect others'?

Ethics is a highly complex subject which would require a much longer book than this one.   We can however isolate, define and elaborate on certain basic axioms.   Noting that no human society, primitive, modern or whatever can *function* as a society without the behavioural rule that human beings should *behave compatibly with each other*, we suggest that this is the 'core principle' of ethics. Human beings *expect* and sometimes *require* each other to behave compatibly, which implies *respect*.

It is not difficult therefore to provide a definition of 'good' (in its moral sense) as follows: *'that which ought to be done or allowed to happen in the interests of others as well as oneself'*. This is a complex definition incorporating an imperative, and it requires some explication. A very similar precept is found in most creeds, belief systems, religions etc. throughout the world; it is comparable to the well-known Golden Rule (treat others as you would wish to be treated), although there are some differences. As we shall see, it does not negate valid self-interest. It could be called the "core moral precept" for short, meaning that if you do something in the interests of others or, at the very least, compatible with the interests of others, it is 'good'. It is the common denominator underlying all moral rules and through it, all obligations, rights, values, moral attitudes and so on are validated or otherwise.

Contrary to a widespread misconception, *values* cannot be the basis of ethics for the simple reason that they are subjective, inconsistent and relative to each other from one society to another and even from one person to another. To avoid going round in circles from one set of value beliefs to another, a criterion is needed *which is not itself a value*. The core moral precept, on the other hand, is not a value, it is a *behavioural rule* which applies to all human beings. It is a necessary condition for any human society of any sort to function, so that as well as having an objectivity which values lack, it is also *obligatory*. This distinguishes it from 'social contract' theories of rights, ethics etc. which, apart from being unduly metaphorical and conjectural, are primarily based upon *agreement*. The core moral precept, by contrast, is about behaving in the interests of others as well as your own because you *have to*. It is a 'mode of behaviour' which is *required* in any human society.

This is why moral *rules* have evolved in human societies. Even with many cultural differences from one society to another (see also *Relativism*, Chapter Six), there are important similarities and certain rules (e.g. against murder, theft, deceit etc.) are almost universal. Such rules are necessary in any human society, and it is mistaken to analyse a statement such as 'it is wrong to tell lies' as 'only' a social convention or 'only' an expression of a personal value belief. The same applies to other moral rules embodying other moral obligations.

Obligation is often equated with *feelings* such as twinges of conscience, or a *sense* of obligation, but this can be misleading. It also has a more objective, generic sense denoting the interplay of all the requests, expectations, requirements, orders, rules, commands, imperatives, instructions and so on that human beings apply to each other for one reason or another. Many of these requirements have no particular moral import (e.g. 'shut the door'), but those that do (e.g. 'do not kill') are, collectively, what constitutes moral obligation. It is important to recognize the objective sense of 'obligation'. It is not purely a question of what you think or feel; it is rooted, ultimately, in what other people *require*. It is similar with *guilt*. Psychologists will correctly characterize guilt as a *feeling* you have (or even a 'complex'), but lawyers, parents, teachers, policemen and many others would add, equally correctly, that guilt has an objective meaning too - you are guilty, as a matter of *fact*, if you have done something you should not have done. Likewise, you can *have an obligation* whether you have a feeling of obligation or not. This is how different people with different values, attitudes, moods, inclinations etc. can be under the *same* obligation(s).

Obligation towards others produces *rights*. If one person has an obligation to another, the other person *acquires* a right as a result. This brings us back to the correlation between rights and obligations which we noted earlier. For example we all have a moral duty to be truthful which is what creates everyone else's right to be told the truth. So if the duty or obligation is validated by the core moral precept in the first place, then the same applies, transitively, to the right. If you have an obligation to respect other people and they have exactly the same obligation to you, that is how you all have the right to be respected. These examples show how rights are *constructs* out of ethical concepts, or *derivatives* from them. This is the basis of rights.

Of course, not all correlations between obligations and rights are reciprocal. Doctors have obligations to provide medical care to their patients who have correlative rights to medical care, but patients do not have obligations to provide medical care to their doctors. A baby has rights to be succoured by its mother, but not *vice versa*. But in general terms, numerous examples of the correlation between obligations and rights, reciprocal or 'one way only', can be found in all sorts of contexts and relationships - personal, moral, legal, social and political. As we have said before, rights are not 'things' which are 'part of what we are'; they are *relational concepts*.

The principal distinction is between *positive* obligations to *do* things and *negative* obligations *not to do* things. These correlate with positive rights and negative rights respectively. For example other people's positive obligations to treat you with reasonable consideration are the basis of your right to be treated with reasonable consideration. Other people's negative obligations *not* to gratuitously annoy you, offend you or harass you are the basis of your rights *not* to be gratuitously annoyed, offended or harassed. The "core moral precept" also underpins a number of very important negative moral obligations - not to deceive, not to murder, not to steal, not to torture and so on, against which our individual rights not to be deceived, murdered etc. are *correlatives* and *valid claims*.

Note that if rights are the correlates of valid obligations we can *infer* and *ascribe* rights even though *claims* for rights may not or cannot be made, as with babies, the absent, the comatose or persons unknown etc.. We shall look at *claims* for rights in more detail in Chapter Three. But once again, it is unnecessary to postulate vague metaphorical notions of 'natural' rights. Babies are not born clutching baby-sized copies of "The Rights of Man" in their baby-sized hands. On the contrary, their rights are based upon the obligations of others (very clear ones, too).

It is naive to ask, why can't there just be rights *without* other people's obligations, irrespective of whether they are based on other people's obligations or not? We answer these questions with another one - what would rights be if they were *not* based on other people's obligations? The answer is very simple: they would not be 'rights' at all. They would be indistinguishable from wants, wishes, hopes, needs, desires or demands which, just in themselves, could mean anything at all. The concept of a *right* would have no distinct meaning, as well as leading us (in theory) to permanent 'rights gridlock' between you, me and everyone else.

Interestingly, there are certain notional or 'imperfect' obligations that do not entail rights which should be mentioned. These include the obligations to be charitable, or to forgive others. We have a moral obligation to be charitable to others if we can, but it does not follow that every charity registered with the Charity Commission is entitled to insist upon donations from us 'as of right'. Maybe we are too poor to give to charity; maybe we have other, pre-existing obligations already. We have a notional moral duty to forgive wrongdoers, but it would be strange if they can claim a *right* to be forgiven for anything more serious than minor misdemeanours. If a wrongdoer has a *right* to be forgiven he would have grounds for complaint if he is *not* forgiven, but if you cannot forgive someone who has seriously wronged you his 'right to be forgiven' would place you, the innocent party, in the wrong which is absurd.   This is why the duty to forgive is not compulsory, it is *discretionary* - otherwise it would not really be forgiveness.

Conversely some rights do not entail obligations by others, specifically *liberty rights* as explained in Chapter One.   To say that I am 'at liberty' in a free country to travel from A to B simply means that I have no duty *not* to go there (or no specific duty to be doing something else), and that is all.   It does not in itself entail that somebody else is obliged to pay my travelling costs, help me get there or do anything at all.   Note that *freedom* is much more complex, as we shall see later on.   But liberties, arising as they do, in many cases, from circumstances, do not in themselves entail obligations by others.

Some general points about ethics need to be made. This is essential for a proper understanding of 'rights'.   Importantly, it is a defining characteristic of moral rules, precepts and obligations that they are always 'universalizable'.   This principle was elaborated by Immanuel Kant (1724-1804) and reiterated in more recent times by R.M. Hare (1919-2002).   Without going into a long exposition, the salient point is that a moral imperative such as 'do not murder', for example, does not simply mean do not murder on this particular occasion, it means do not murder on *any* occasion.   A moral *rule* is not the same as an *ad hoc* request or command.   By contrast, many non-moral imperatives such as 'shut the door' or 'don't pick the daisies' tend not to be based upon universal rules (although some are, such as 'don't drink sulphuric acid').

Universalizability of meaning is implicit in all moral codes and it entails, among other things, one very important principle: because moral rules must be applied universally, it is *wrong* to be inconsistent and to treat people arbitrarily, for example to be 'moral' to people you like but not to people you don't like. It will be appreciated that this is very relevant to rights, implying the importance of *objectivity* and *impartiality* which are necessary conditions for *justice*.

But universalizability must not be interpreted over-rigidly. The "core moral precept" carries certain provisos - in particular, it must exclude any actions that are 'bad'. It is right that we should help others, for example, but it is not right to help someone hurting or harming someone *else*. Moral precepts must be 'universalizable' in the sense that they must apply universally, but this does not mean that their *formulation* should not incorporate provisos, conditions and so on. Clearly a definition of 'bad' or 'wrong' is also required, namely: '*that which must not be done or allowed to happen as a cause of hurt or harm to others*'. This carries certain provisos too, for example it is not a wrong if I suffer the 'hurt' of being penalized for wilfully or negligently hurting others. Likewise it is not a wrong for violent and dangerous individuals to be deprived of their liberty so as to keep everyone else safe, as we have said before (see also *Crime and Punishment*, Chapter Six).

Another point is that in very exceptional circumstances, it is not always wrong to hurt someone deliberately. If you are defending yourself against violent attack and you hurt your attacker, you may feel disinclined to think that you have acted wrongly at all. It is not wrong to fight in the defence of your country if you are invaded, otherwise a much greater wrong will result (invaders don't usually bother to respect people's human rights). It is often impossible to defend yourself effectively without hurting your attacker to a greater or lesser extent, and if you are morally prohibited from doing so then self-defence is a moral wrong. This gives your attacker a false moral advantage by default, and an ethic with this result is paradoxical in theory and dysfunctional in practice (pacifists please note). It is accepted that every sovereign state has a right to maintain armed forces for defensive purposes.

The point is that 'in the interests of others' must not be interpreted *exclusively*. Don't forget your own interests. Self-interest is also necessary in life's rough-and-tumble, and we are not saying 'in the interests of others *instead of* yourself', we are saying '*as well as*'. This distinction is of cardinal importance. We are *not* talking about altruism, and you can be self-interested without necessarily being selfish or morally wrong. The major problem with altruism is that if it literally means acting in the interests of others *instead of* yourself this excludes by definition the validity of self-defence (as noted above), as well as ruling out the validity of standing up for yourself in any context whatsoever which is merely absurd.

But the core moral precept, on the other hand, *implies* self-interest in the sense of *being responsible for yourself.* It is not 'in the interests of others' if you fail to make adequate arrangements for your own interests etc. if you are capable of doing so. This is, in fact, an important obligation you have towards others. Of course, other people have duties and responsibilities towards you and you depend upon other people for all sorts of things. But this is a matter of degree. If you are an adult of usual capabilities you are expected to look after yourself, most of the time. It is only different if you are very young, very old, disabled, ill or have suffered serious misfortune or injustice.

It is also a mistake to misinterpret 'good = in the interests of others' to mean that if something is not in the interests of others then it is necessarily 'bad'. This would exclude the validity of *competition* which means, literally, to compete against the interests of someone else. So, how does economic competition, for example, square with acting in the interests of others as well as oneself? The answer is that 'in the interests of others' in its moral sense is primarily concerned to exclude hurt or harm to the *person*, damage to or theft of *property*, and *dishonesty*. It does not, therefore, exclude fair competition. It *does* exclude dishonest trading and/or exploitation of workers. Analogously, consider the difference in sport between fair play and foul. And insofar as fair competition is a necessary condition for economic growth and development, it brings clear benefits which make it morally valid.

The core moral precept can be broadened and adapted to actions, events etc. in purely *general* terms, so that a generalized definition of 'good' would be *beneficial*. Judgment is required in different circumstances as to whether attention should be focused on the interests or concerns of all human beings, most human beings, a few human beings or particular human beings. Moral dilemmas can arise that are not easy, and the most we can do is to summarize a few guidelines. It is only commonsense for example to assess the consequences of our decisions and actions, but we can only do this so far and it is misleading to determine the right thing to do purely in terms of consequences. It is important to avoid the 'end justifies the means' syndrome which can often provide a spurious 'justification' for the most wicked of acts in the name of some glorious ideal or other important objective.

Defining 'good' as 'beneficial' lies behind the 'utilitarian' concept of equating 'good' with 'the greatest happiness of the greatness number of people'. Apart from involving various formulation difficulties, utilitarianism is often regarded by its critics as objectionable because the rights of the individual are potentially diminished, not noticed or lost altogether. Maybe so, but sometimes it is equally 'objectionable' to place the individual on a moral pedestal. Which individual are you talking about - Tom, Dick or Harriet, who are harmless enough, or somebody much more sinister?

The key question is, how do you decide between one person's concerns and interests and another's? Part of the answer lies in the comparative harm principle as already discussed. There are different *degrees* of hurt or harm, and we can observe and differentiate between the severe, serious, medium, moderate or minimal. Few people find it difficult to distinguish between the seriousness of major deception, for example, at one end of the 'dishonesty' scale and telling fibs at the other. Both are wrong but to different degrees. We therefore have *moral appraisal* and *perspective*, making it possible to assess whether an action or event will be directly and severely harmful to another person or less so. These principles are central to determining which right and whose right should take priority in particular situations.

Some further points about ethics need to be made. In particular, it is very important to distinguish between moral, natural and accidental hurts or harms. These are standard distinctions within moral theory, as well as plain commonsense. To be murdered is a *wrong*; to die from a serious illness is *natural*. If you are struck by lightning or hit by a car whose driver has just had a heart attack, these are *accidents*. If we classify all hurts and harms as 'wrongs' irrespective of how they are caused, then it would be impossible to make a moral distinction between being murdered and dying of a serious illness, between losing something and being robbed, and so on. We would also end up with naive and equivocal ideas on all sorts of other issues, as we shall see later on. Rights abuse and injustice occur when hurts or harms are deliberately or negligently caused by others, but they do not occur, obviously, with *naturally caused* hurts or harms such as illness or being struck by lightning. These are *misfortunes*, not wrongs which have been perpetrated by others.

Of course, people have clear moral duties to seek to rectify or alleviate the sufferings of others resulting from accidents, disease etc., and negligence is a moral wrong.   But there are also limits upon what people can reasonably be expected to do.   Nobody can do the impossible; if you can't swim you can't save a drowning man and you are not held to blame for that.   If you are poor, you can't give very much to charity.   Even governments cannot do everything they ought (in theory) to do.   The *scope* of what we can or should do has limitations too. Under normal, non-urgent circumstances people are only expected in everyday life to have very general, non-specific responsibilities towards people outside of their own circle of relationships.

Moving on, the word 'right' is ambiguous, of course.   There is an important distinction between *having a right* to do something and *the right thing to do*.   These do not always mean the same thing. For example an employer has rights to promote an employee, to give her a pay rise, to dismiss her or to do nothing in particular, but *the right thing to do* in one situation or another depends upon circumstances and other factors (e.g. the law, employees' rights, and so on).   Likewise if you are married you have the right in the UK to seek a divorce, but the right thing to do will depend upon all sorts of complex and difficult considerations. In both of these very different examples, the point of principle is the same - there may be a right to do something but it could be the wrong thing to do, or a bad thing to do.   A married couple are *within their rights* to get divorced but this might compromise their children's needs for a stable, cohesive family life. It follows that the right thing to do is often a more fundamental question than having a right, and having a right does not always or necessarily *make* something the right thing to do, or a sensible thing to do.

This is commonly misunderstood, another of those awkward little details which many people do not notice or gloss over. *Rights fixation* can be very misleading, easily prone to muddle, confusion and sometimes to other wrongs. It is often assumed that if you have a right to do something, that is final. But sometimes it is very far from 'final'. You might think you can't be in the wrong so long as you're 'within your rights', but you can. Likewise there is no moral or logical incongruity in saying that I have a right to free speech but I am in the wrong if I slander others. That is because both of these statements are *true*. There is only an *apparent* inconsistency if you conflate a right (which is an *option*) and an action (which is an *event*). There is no inconsistency in saying that you have a *right* to do X in general terms but that your *action* X on a particular occasion was wrong.[1]

---

[1] Otherwise, if it is inconsistent to say that 'I have a right to free speech but I am in the wrong to slander others' then *either* it is not wrong to slander others, which is false (otherwise *you* have no right not to be slandered by *me*), *or* I have no right to free speech which is also false. Either way, we are led to false conclusions. Therefore the premise of the argument, that it is inconsistent to say that I have a right to free speech but I am in the wrong to slander others, is false. Q.E.D.

On the other hand, *having a right* to do something and *the right thing to do* can validly coincide, and *will* coincide, if a *morally overriding right* is at stake. Moral codes in most human societies place specific emphasis on rules against *deliberate harm to the person* (e.g. murder, malicious injury, unprovoked attack, rape, torture) which correlate with 'morally overriding rights' against such actions. These rights *can* be the sole justifying reasons for an action. The right to self-defence is a very obvious example. Other rights, for example your rights not to be robbed or not to be deceived, are also morally overriding because of their importance, but not necessarily to the same degree as your rights to personal safety. Infringement of your right not to be deceived may be a sufficient reason for seeking divorce, but not for taking violent action.

Rights can however cease to be overriding in exceptional circumstances and it is possible to forfeit a right. These are issues we have encountered before, of course. There is a very important right not to be deceived, but if you are seeking to murder someone it is not a wrong if another person (who knows your intentions) deceives you as to your intended victim's whereabouts. Your right not to be insulted is important, but if you have seriously wronged someone do not be surprised if they say things to you that are less than complimentary. You have rights not to be injured by others but if you attack someone, do not be surprised if they fight back - and who is to say they are acting wrongly? Rights do not necessarily provide you with moral protection or moral indemnity against actions which others might rightfully take against you.

Three - Interests, Rights and Claims for Rights

The most basic needs of all human beings for food, shelter, clothing, medical care etc. are *life-critical*. Therefore to deny or to neglect these needs is a major wrong, otherwise a serious harm is suffered. This particularly applies to those with special needs, e.g. the very poor, the disabled, the ill or injured, and so on; the very young and the very old require special attention too. There are moral duties to avert hurts or harms to others and to alleviate suffering, particularly in urgent situations.

Of course, we can say perfectly clearly that it is wrong to neglect the life-critical needs of others whether we talk in terms of *rights* or not. So, where exactly do rights come in? The *right* is that a morally valid need or interest should not be denied or neglected *without a morally valid reason for doing so*. Rights are said to give 'moral protection' to valid needs or interests - the key word being 'valid' which excludes 'needs and interests' which cause serious hurt or harm to others. The question of a right to kill does not even arise with a serial killer's 'need' to kill.

In general terms 'needs' and 'interests' have different nuances of meaning, of course, with some overlap. Both can be 'valid' or otherwise; both can be 'prospective', and both depend to varying extents upon other people. Sometimes they entail obligations by others, sometimes not. But although rights are often *about* needs and/or interests, it is a common mistake to *equate* rights with needs or interests or to draw certain false conclusions. I need food, clothing and so on and I have certain rights, but this does not mean that the world owes me a living. I have a legitimate interest in being promoted at work, but that does not in itself give me the *right* to be promoted. You may aspire to political power, maybe for very good and honourable reasons, but having a *right* to political power depends upon various other considerations (winning an election, for example). Conversely, rights can be *unrelated* to your needs or interests. If your job validly requires you to give advice then you have a right to give advice for that reason alone.

Needs and rights are not the *same*. Otherwise, I could say "oh, how I need a holiday in the sunshine!" and lo and behold, I have a right to a holiday in the sunshine. Very nice too, and there is nothing wrong with holidays in the sunshine. But not all rights entail claims against others and it does not follow that if I can't afford a holiday in the sunshine somebody else is obliged to pay for it and that it infringes my rights if they don't. It is facile to have a 'magic wand' perception of rights where all you have to do is to 'assert' a need and hey presto, you have a *right* and equally 'hey presto', other people are suddenly landed with a range of obligations they never knew they had. This only leads to 'obligation overload', as we have noted before.

Returning to life-critical needs which are more serious than holidays in the sunshine, even here there are difficulties. Moral protection of needs or interests does not, unfortunately, mean 'entitled to guaranteed delivery' in practical terms, and there are two valid reasons for 'failure to deliver', namely *valid refusal* or *inability* to give, provide, supply etc.. This needs to be looked at in detail.

Under normal circumstances people are expected to cater for their own needs and interests, other things being equal. Failure to pay for food or other goods ordinarily entails valid refusal by others to provide them, whether our needs are life critical or not. It is only different in urgent and exceptional circumstances, as in impoverished Third World countries where the necessity for *aid* is extremely serious. There are moral obligations upon others not to be negligent, but a major problem is that sometimes the obligations of others can be *limited* in practical, substantive terms through inability and/or incapacity, in particular considerations of cost and scarcity of resources which cannot always be helped. The government of an impoverished country may not have the resources to feed its own population. Unless its officials are guilty of corruption and so on, it cannot be blamed, so in what sense are there rights to something which cannot be given for genuine, *bona fide* reasons?

Many people, charities and governments seek to give aid for starving people in Third World countries because there are moral duties of care for others as well as the obligation not to be negligent. It is usually only governments and large charities that have the resources to address the problem with all its administrative and political side-issues. But critics of foreign aid argue that a lot of donated money ends up in the pockets of corrupt politicians, so it is argued that the obligation to provide aid is questionable and there are other complications too.

Sceptics also ask how the obligation is to be defined in *practical* terms, and *whose* obligation is it? If the Universal Declaration of Human Rights says that all human beings should have rights to housing, healthcare, nutrition and other benefits, unless it specifies *who* has the obligation and with what resources to provide these benefits then the rights are not so much false as *incompletely defined.* This is because the *location of accountability* is undefined, which has ramifications too. Some might suggest that everybody else has the obligation 'in global terms', but in a practical, specific sense this is, likewise, indeterminate. But where does all this leave the right (if any) of poor people to aid? It could be argued that we are not really talking about rights at all, and is it morally responsible to tell poor people that they have rights to goods and benefits whose provision is far from certain? Also, what if too much emphasis on rights to aid engenders a dependency culture? The same question, incidentally, applies to the provision of social benefits in the West.

These are cogent arguments, but none of them invalidate the *moral* obligation to care for those who need it. And this, of course, is why many in the West seek to alleviate Third World Poverty. Therefore, despite the scepticism there are still *moral rights* to aid. However - those who work in charities, foreign aid etc. can only do their best with limited resources, so it is not always possible to impute negligence or to claim infringement of rights.

Similar issues occur closer to home with the National Health Service of the UK, but there are some differences. Firstly, though, the similarities - there can be no obligation upon anyone, not even governments, to do the genuinely impossible, and the UK National Health Service is financially unable to provide *all* the medical equipment, new drugs etc. to everyone who needs them. The UK national budget is not infinite. There is a *moral* right to health care, but it does not follow from this that there is a *substantive* right, if it cannot be met. So where does this leave the right of UK citizens to free medical care at the point of delivery? The NHS has only limited resources which can never cater for the *un*limited needs of the population, so its obligation is *contingent* through force of circumstances. The right to free medical care at the point of delivery is therefore a *contingent* right. And because the obligation is limited through force of circumstances, it is not the same as a deliberate infringement of rights or a dereliction of duty.

However, an important difference between medical care under the NHS and the previous example of foreign aid is that many NHS patients have, to a certain extent, *paid for* the NHS themselves via taxation. They could say, 'I've paid my tax and insurance contributions like most other people so I have certain rights'. But there is no ability to enforce these rights in law; they are indeterminate, and if NHS resources are limited then substantive rights to specific treatments may be limited too, although the moral rights are clear.

In these circumstances the NHS has a duty to be particularly careful over dealing with patients *equitably*. For example there *is* an infringement of rights if scarce or expensive drugs etc. are not distributed equitably between different people who need them. Thus there are complaints over 'post-code lotteries'. Likewise, in 2006 a group of women suffering from breast cancer had to mount a campaign to receive the expensive Herceptin drug. This was approved by the National Institute for Health and Clinical Excellence, but a few months later it was reported that the provision of drugs arresting early stage Alzheimer's disease was to be denied on grounds of cost.

This created the unfortunate impression that NHS patients can acquire rights to expensive drugs if they are able to *make a fuss*, but if not, not. People suffering from Alzheimer's disease cannot normally go on protest marches. This suggests an *ad hoc*, almost 'populist' approach to health care by the NHS, not helped by a bifurcation of responsibility on many questions between NICE and the NHS trusts. With an ill-defined location of accountability, therefore, patients' rights will be ill-defined too. Possibly the ultimate responsibility lies with the government, but on this question it is likely that we will merely be redirected to NICE and the NHS trusts.....

To summarize, if obligations are clear and unequivocal then the correlative rights will be clear and unequivocal too. But if the obligations are ill-defined, ambiguous, indeterminate, limited, contingent etc. then, although the moral rights are perfectly clear, the substantive rights will be *equally* ill-defined, ambiguous, contingent etc.. We mentioned in Chapter One how substantive rights can be contingent. It is not always possible therefore to impute blame in the event of failure to deliver. Rights to foreign aid or to health care under the NHS can only be *contingent* rights because the obligations are *contingent* through *force of circumstances*. Declarations about human rights can only mean *moral* rights, not substantive rights, if goods, services, benefits etc. are limited. And as we have seen, *needs* and *rights* are not, unfortunately, the same thing, and the reader will recall the imperfect obligations noted in the last chapter. These will only correlate with 'imperfect' rights.

Often, the location of accountability is indeterminate (and sometimes contentious). The *right to work* is complex because the location of accountability is split three ways. Governments are generally expected to maintain (as far as they can) such economic and fiscal conditions as will enable trade and employment to be maintained. Individuals are expected to try to find work if they need to work and are capable of working. Employers requiring labour are expected to pay for it (equitably), not to refuse employment to job applicants for invalid reasons and to provide adequate training. But whether there is a right to work or not, employers cannot be expected to create vacancies artificially. If they were, the additional cost overheads would force many of them out of business making even more people unemployed. So for all sorts of reasons, the right to work is contingent and conditional upon multifarious factors which laws or government policies cannot easily change.

Your right to keep your job, slightly differently, raises other questions too. In legal terms (in the

UK) there is no such right, strictly speaking - it is more accurate to say that you have rights not to be dismissed *unfairly*.   In certain circumstances you can be fairly dismissed for pretty obvious reasons, e.g. for refusal to follow valid instructions.   But you can also be fairly dismissed neither through any fault of your own nor through culpable rights infringement on the part of your employer, for example if staffing levels have to be reduced for economic reasons, or if your employer has to close down altogether.   In such situations it is difficult to ascribe blame.   Economic circumstances are often beyond anyone's control, and your employer has no more wish to close down than you have to be thrown out of work.

However, in many areas of life the principle of *compensation for losses* is well established. Although for economic reasons your employer cannot help having to reduce employee numbers or to close down, the fact remains that if you are made redundant you lose your rights to the salary you were paid and maybe to other benefits as well. But in many countries there are statutory rights to redundancy payments and to fair selection for redundancy.   These are *residual,* or *compensatory,* rights.

Rather differently, but in some ways comparably, residual rights also arise if a promise has not been kept for one reason or another.   If you fail to keep a promise you are liable because of the effect of your default upon the interests of others, even if this is through circumstances beyond your control.   In legal contexts a default is a default, irrespective of the reasons for it, and in moral contexts it is similar.

For example you promised to take your daughter to the theatre but you cannot because your mother has fallen ill.   This is not your fault, and your daughter is unlikely to sue you or to complain that her rights have been infringed.   But your obligation towards her is not negated or 'deleted'; you have a *residual* obligation to take her out on another occasion which would correlate with *residual* rights on her part.

But sometimes liability does not arise at all.   For example you have a moral claim-right for others to save you from being hurt or harmed in perilous situations because there is a moral duty of care incumbent upon everyone.   If we go mountaineering and there is a huge boulder about to fall on your head, I have a moral duty to prevent this from happening *if I can*, but not if I cannot. Maybe I'm too far away to do anything; maybe you cannot hear my shouts.   Claim-rights can sometimes be frustrated by circumstances, lack of ability etc. that no-one is accountable for.   If I fail to save you it is not a culpable infringement of your rights and I am not liable.

Likewise, consider your right to medical care as provided by a doctor if you are extremely ill.   You have rights that doctors should do their best in terms of their expertise, available medical facilities etc. and you have rights that they should not be negligent in carrying out their duties (medical ethics and legal requirements are very precise on the responsibilities of doctors and nurses).   But subject to such criteria being met, the fact remains that if your condition is so serious that you cannot be cured there is no liability on the part of medical staff if you die.

Concluding this chapter, it is important to distinguish between a *claim* and a *right*. The expression 'claim-right' amalgamates part of what is meant by a claim with part of what is meant by a right. Many important, general rights (e.g. the right not to be lied to) are 'established' and are directly based on pre-existing moral imperatives. It can be different with more specific rights where particular *criteria* may apply. In many cases it is possible to claim a right subject to well-defined conditions, for example your winning lottery ticket, duly signed by yourself together with ID, enables you to claim and to have a right to your prize very straightforwardly. Your claim is valid because it meets the *relevant criteria*.

Claims for rights can sometimes be invalid, though. If you claim a right to a higher salary, this will be difficult to maintain if your existing salary is comparable to that of your colleagues, if your work output is no greater than theirs, if the work you do is no more complex or demanding than theirs and if you are all paid salaries that are fully competitive with pay-rates in the labour market generally and are in line with the cost of living. It is a claim that fails to meet the *relevant criteria*. Conversely, if it meets any (or all) of the relevant criteria, you have a reasonable case for negotiation, under normal circumstances.

Now consider a valid but protracted claim for women's rights within the political dimension. Before 1918 women in the UK did not have the right to vote. There was no law that gave them that right, so there was no legal obligation they could claim against.   In essence, their argument could only be formulated in moral terms (plus some practical action).   Votes for women could not, obviously, be considered unethical or morally wrong, or inappropriate, nor could there be any practical objections such as cost of implementation. The Suffragettes were therefore claiming a right which met all the *criteria* for having a right, substantively as well as morally.

Some theorists characterize rights as *valid claims*, but the stress needs to be placed on '*valid*'.   A claim is a *process*, of course - it has a beginning and an *end*, or an *outcome*.   A claim only *becomes* a right in the fullest sense if it meets the relevant criteria in a particular case, which must include an *identifiable*, *determinate* and *feasible* obligation by another party to give or provide what is claimed. It is only when these various criteria are met that a claim can become a *right*.   But without such criteria it is impossible to differentiate between valid claims and invalid claims.   Claims can sometimes be mistaken, or spurious.   It is misleading to characterize rights as 'claims' pure and simple, or to use the terms interchangeably as some theorists seem to do.   A claim is not a right as such.   Otherwise, rights would be indistinguishable from wants, desires or *ad hoc* demands.

But as we have also seen, there can be moral rights based upon the moral obligations of others but which are 'imperfect' through the inability or limited ability of others to *provide*.   And this can happen, unfortunately, with some very important rights, as with aid, health care services or the right to work.   Although written declarations on rights play an important role in highlighting the importance of certain rights, they cannot function as *guarantees* in practical terms.

Four - Liberty, Freedom and Prerogatives

Very broadly, there are two types of freedom: (i) freedom *from* bad, undesirable things such as hunger, illness, persecution, discrimination, murder, attack etc. and (ii) freedom *to do* things which are in line with valid objectives such as to speak freely, associate freely, to work, trade, get educated, travel and so on. We could call these (i) 'passive' freedoms and (ii) 'active' freedoms respectively.

In many ways we have already discussed 'passive' freedoms - in a different form of words. Freedom *from* hurts or harms is co-extensive in meaning with negative claim-rights that you should not be hurt or harmed. Likewise freedom from hunger, illness etc. is co-extensive in meaning with positive claim-rights to medical care, aid, and so on. We have already explored the main issues and difficulties involved, although *discrimination* will be discussed separately in the next chapter.

In this chapter we concentrate mainly on the 'active' freedoms to do things. It is always in the interests of human beings that they should enjoy a full range of personal freedoms, these being necessary conditions for valid human objectives to be realized. Specific examples of freedom include the rights to trade, to travel, to privacy, to freedom of speech, to freedom of assembly, to academic freedom and to many other freedoms. Modern society would be impossible without freedom. It is the basis, at root, of growth and development in the economic sphere and we have already referred to the moral validity and necessity for economic competition. This is impossible without freedom.

Freedom is accordingly very broad in its scope, ranging from the personal dimension to economics and to international politics.

In practical terms *interference with freedom* can have a very major impact on the lives of individuals and even on an entire society. The right to travel is an interesting example because it is taken for granted by modern Westerners. For there was only limited freedom to travel within the Soviet Union whose citizens needed official permission to travel from one city to another *within their own country* (let alone to travel abroad). Cities such as Karaganda, Gorky etc. were off-limits altogether, and Soviet peasants were not granted internal passports until 1982. The over-regimented Soviet economy was hardly a success story either. The right of free speech did not exist, and if you criticized the regime you could be arrested and sent to a forced labour camp (or, in Stalin's time, shot). You could also have the secret police banging on your door at 4.00am to take you off to execution without trial, the fate of millions of people in the Soviet Union during the "Great Terror" in the 1930's.

But how do we *define* 'freedom'? Firstly, although the words 'liberty' and 'freedom' are often used interchangeably they are *different*, albeit with frequent overlap. Reiterating the summary given earlier, a *liberty* exists if an action is neither compulsory or prohibited, or if there is no valid duty to be doing something else. It is a free country and Julia is *at liberty* to travel from A to B. There are no laws against it. She may sometimes be prevented from doing so by other commitments such as her job, but otherwise she is at liberty to travel wherever she likes - and that is all it means. For that matter she is 'at liberty' to fly to Mars. There are no laws against it. But she is not *free* to fly to Mars because she *cannot*.

Liberty rights are completely different from *claim-rights*, which correlate with the obligations of others. My liberty to travel from A to B does not correlate with anyone else's *obligation*; no-one is obliged to take me there or help me get there just because I fancy going there. A liberty does not entail claim-rights against anyone. It exists 'by default', in the absence of duties or obligations *not to do* something.

Freedom has a 'stand-alone' status which is very different from *liberty* just on its own. For although liberty is not a claim-right (and does not entail claim-rights against anyone else), there is no reason why a liberty cannot be *conjoined* with a claim-right. Therefore, as many theorists do, we shall define freedom as a combination of both a *liberty right* and a *claim-right against interference*. Freedom is therefore a *complex right*. In this sense, my right to travel from A to B correlates with a duty of others *not to interfere* with that right *so long as I am not doing something I should not be doing* (e.g. attempting to travel by train without a ticket or driving a stolen car). Thus, there is a moral claim-right against interference *conditional* upon there being no valid obligation not to be doing something. There is a permanent tension, obviously, between the two elements, but this is the basic definition of *freedom*. As we shall see, it has further components too.

Interference, of course, can often be perfectly innocuous such as a trivial interruption and as we shall see in a moment, it is important to distinguish between interference and valid intervention. It is more accurate to talk of *unwarranted* interference, especially malicious interference such as being arrested and shot without valid cause in a totalitarian state. The right to freedom is therefore a very important right. However, in general terms it is conditional: the main *proviso* on freedom rights is that you have an obligation to respect the rights of others. If you do not, then other people no longer have a duty not to interfere with your freedoms but maybe the opposite. And life itself consists to a considerable extent of having to do things you don't want to do and not doing things you'd like to do. If your spouse wants you to help with the washing up, if your employer wants you to be at work on time, these are not infringements of your right to freedom.

It is therefore impossible to define freedom as the right not to be interfered with just on its own. That is why it incorporates the meaning of *liberty* which is always conditional upon there being no valid duty *not* to do something or no valid duty to be doing something *else*. To complicate matters further, people sometimes have a right to *intervene* in the freedom of others, a prerogative right (see below) which we all have otherwise we couldn't even request someone to do or not to do something. It is also necessary to instruct, demand, insist, goad, guide, interrupt, forbid and, in broader contexts, to regulate.

What is law enforcement if it is not society's *right to intervene* with those of its members whose activities threaten and infringe the rights of others? There are important differences of meaning between 'intervention' and 'interference', but both have one major factor in common, namely prohibiting, preventing or stopping someone from doing something. Also, if *ethics* means anything at all it must be morally permissible to intervene (or 'interfere') with the actions of people who contravene the rights of others. This must sometimes be obligatory, and if this is impermissible through a dogmatically interpreted duty of others 'not to interfere' then an anti-social person acquires a liberty right *by default* to behave anti-socially. It is also necessary, sometimes, to use force (try restraining a violent drunken person without using a modicum of 'force'....).

Laws and rules have evolved in human societies to prohibit and to rectify anti-social behaviour (both major and minor). Rather like rain-clouds, rules are necessary features of human existence and it is not difficult to see why. Willingly or otherwise, human beings exist as members of societies but, as individuals, human beings are prone to be *selfish*. This can range from merely being inconsiderate at one end of the scale through to the grossest infringements of the rights of others at the extreme end of the scale, e.g. murder. Regulation of human behaviour by rules has always therefore been a necessary feature of human life, and probably always will be. Rules, however, need to be observed and adhered to and therefore enforced, otherwise lots of people will take no notice of them (people are like that). This means sanctions of one sort or another, heartily disliked by anarchists, reformers, adolescents, idealists, criminals, psychopaths and the editors of certain newspapers, but no society is possible in the real world without them.

Not following valid rules, either deliberately or through negligence, can adversely affect the rights and freedoms of others. This can happen in all sorts of contexts. Driving through a red light or ignoring other traffic rules can potentially cause major injuries or fatalities. Crime, of any sort, is not following rules. Telling lies is not following rules. Of course, we are not talking about *any* rules (which can be arbitrary); we mean rules that are 'underwritten', ultimately, by moral rules.

Valid rules are designed to protect your rights and freedoms against unwarranted incursions by others. Like lubricating oil, rules enable the rights of different individuals to mesh together. In this way they do not inhibit your freedom, they enhance it. We have therefore defined *structured freedom*, or the well known concept of *ordered liberty*, as distinct from anarchy at one extreme or totalitarianism at the other. We end up, really, with a 'Ming vase' concept of freedom - it is very precious but very fragile, and you can lose it if you don't handle it carefully.

Anarchy, of course, is the complete absence of laws, rules and other constraints where human beings murder, rape, loot and pillage at will. It occasionally occurs in the aftermath of wars, revolutions etc. and it is extremely unpleasant. Anarch*ism*, on the other hand, is the theoretical ideal that if all human beings fully respected each other's rights and interests then authority, laws and social rules would be unnecessary. This is only another way of saying that if human beings were like angels society would be a little more like heaven, a purely vapid observation of no practical or even theoretical import whatever. We should also mention that freedom does not mean having a casual, do as you like, take it or leave it attitude to valid rules, conventions or laws. This is an adolescent misinterpretation of a uniquely important concept.

But now we look at the third component of 'freedom'. A *prerogative right*, sometimes called a *power right*, is the discretion to alter the rights and liabilities either of yourself or someone else. Subject to circumstances, this makes *you* the initiating agent in relation to others. For example Julia the Sales Manager has the right to instruct Alice the Sales Representative to make immediate phone calls to all customers who haven't placed orders for three months or more. Alice is now *accountable* for making these calls. Julia also has the discretion to transfer her own responsibility for the more important accounts by delegating them to Alice, who is competent enough to handle them. This leaves Julia free to develop new accounts to keep the business expanding - one of *her* responsibilities.

The term 'power right' is appropriate when the ability to enforce is present (e.g. through legal proceedings etc.) or where your decision cannot be altered by anyone else, for example no-one can prevent you from resigning from your job if that is what you have decided to do. Prerogatives are somewhat weaker and are not necessarily enforceable at law.

It is quite normal for prerogative rights to arise within the context of more or less any relationship, the object being to change the way other people behave. People exercise this right all the time, sometimes validly, sometimes invalidly. Human relationships set parameters, sometimes agreed to, sometimes not, concerning what people are expected to do, not expected to do, required to do, not required to do, free to do, not free to do, and so on. People seek to modify their own and each other's liabilities and rights as circumstances arise. It is often a 'two-way street', but not always. As Sales Manager Julia has prerogatives over what Alice does as a Sales Representative, but this is not reciprocal. There will be consultation for obvious reasons, but Alice does not have *prerogatives* over what Julia does. This is because human organizations, large or small, can only function through *structured* and *differentiated* prerogatives from one person to another.

Prerogative rights are often inherent in people's roles. Parents have these rights to guide, instruct, set examples, advise, persuade, praise, encourage, reward, admonish or sometimes to punish. Teachers, police officers, social workers and many others have prerogative and power rights of very different sorts over the rights and liabilities of other people, and other people do not have the same powers or prerogatives as they do. In many cases these rights cannot normally be pre-empted by anyone else. In the workplace, under normal circumstances only Julia has the right to give Alice instructions; within the UK and other democracies, only the electorate has the valid power to bring a different political party to office.   In certain cases, prerogatives are yours 'as of right'.   Only you have the prerogative to forgive or not to forgive someone who has wronged you.   Only you have the prerogative to release someone from a promise they have made to you.

The distribution of political power and prerogatives within a society can be fair or unfair, as with the power right to vote in elections.   For example it was not reasonable that before 1929, women under 30 were denied the right to vote in the UK.   But it *is* reasonable that although children are expected to know the difference between right and wrong by the age of ten if not earlier, they are not expected to know enough about the world around them to vote until they are quite a few years older.

Prerogative rights can often alter and sometimes override other rights.   This is their specific purpose.   Whilst they cannot override *morally overriding rights*, they can override many liberty rights and claim-rights.   A man and wife have various claim-rights against each other, but each has the prerogative, individually, to instigate divorce proceedings which can replace their existing rights and liabilities by very different ones.   You have the prerogative to instruct your child to leave the cat alone which restricts his 'liberty' to that extent.

Of course, many power and prerogative rights can be questioned or challenged by others for valid reasons, and some may only exist in the first place subject to the assent of others (e.g. by virtue of the job or position which you hold). More importantly, they are also subject to legal, social and moral limitations. Julia has no legal or moral ability to instruct Alice to do anything illegal or unethical, either in her job or in any other capacity. Because Alice is required to comply with the law and to be a responsible person, she has various liabilities and obligations which must not be altered invalidly by a third party. This gives her another kind of right which theorists call an *immunity right*, i.e. a right which arises from the legal or moral *inabilities* of others within a given set of rules to alter the rights or liabilities of others. *Immunity rights* add a further element to the concept of freedom.

As well as various organizational constraints, Julia is fully aware of the legal and moral limitations to her power and prerogative rights, nor is she the sort of person who 'pulls rank'. It should be noted that outside of this neat and tidy textbook example, people in the real world can be confronted with major dilemmas when those to whom they are beholden exercise their power and prerogative rights invalidly.

Within the political dimension the power rights of elected governments in modern democracies are more limited than the powers possessed by the absolute monarchies of the past, or by the totalitarian governments of more recent times. There is *power*, but it is circumscribed by *accountability*. In a modern democracy, governmental *freedom to act* is not an absolute right, it is conditional, the condition being exactly the same as applies to individuals, groups of individuals and to other organizations. This is simply that the right-holder should respect the rights of others, which in the political dimension means refraining from interfering with the rights of others to exercise their own prerogatives, as well as their various other rights.

We conclude this brief study of freedom by returning to *liberty*. Liberty rights have two variants - privileges and permissions, both slightly different from liberties but their 'inner logic' is just the same. For example, under normal circumstances Alice has a duty *not* to make use of other people's property without their prior permission, but if the permission or authorization is granted a privilege is created. Thus Alice is *privileged* to use the telephone at work for the occasional private call. This is different from a claim-right. If a claim-right is infringed the right-holder can always claim against the obligation(s) of the other party. Alice can complain and bring suit if her salary is not paid, but if a privilege is withdrawn there is no such entitlement. She can only express regret if the concession on private calls is discontinued; it is not hers 'as of right'. Permissions are subject to the discretion of others.

Take another example. Nobody has the right of entry to Julia's home without her prior permission. But when she invites Jonathan to dinner, he has the privilege to enter which other people do not, and which he has on just this one occasion. However, he is not thereby entitled to help himself to drinks without being invited to do so. This is known as taking liberties (particularly on a first visit). This simple example from social etiquette is relevant in all sorts of other contexts - moral, legal or political. The fact that you have a liberty in one situation does not entitle you to assume that you have liberties in others, nor do liberties entail claim-rights. As we have explained, they are entirely different.

However, one of the most complex variations of *freedom* is the 'permitted option'. This is where a *permission* is augmented by a claim-right against the obligations of others that you should have this permission 'as of right', not simply through having it at the discretion of others. An example is the right which a married person has in the UK to seek divorce. This is an *option* but it is not one which you just 'happen to have' in the absence of *duties not* to seek divorce. It is made *specific*, and many of the rights specified in the legal systems of democratic societies itemize literally in black and white the various *options* which we are permitted by law to exercise.

At this stage we can summarize *four* basic types of rights:-

- claim-rights
- liberty rights
- power (or prerogative) rights
- immunity rights.

They are all called 'rights' yet each has a clearly distinct meaning:-

A *claim-right* is where a duty is owed to you, or there is an obligation towards you, on the part of another person or persons.

A *liberty right* exists in the absence of any duty or obligation on your part *to do* or *not to do* something, i.e. any action which is neither compulsory nor prohibited but which you are *at liberty* to do or not do.

A *power right* or *prerogative right* is where you have the discretion (i.e. *ability* within a given set of rules) to alter either your own or another's liability and/or rights in a given situation.

An *immunity right* arises from the legal or moral inabilities of *others* within a given set of rules to do something that would alter *your* rights and/or liabilities.

Although each type of right has its own distinct meaning, they can be combined to give *complex rights*, for example 'freedom' combines all four in varying combinations from one situation to another. 'Ownership', also very complex, likewise combines claim-rights, liberties, prerogatives and immunities.

This fourfold classification of rights was drawn up by Wesley Newcomb Hohfeld (1879-1918), a Yale University law professor who identified misleading ambiguities in how the concept of a right was employed within legal contexts. Some rights clearly involved claims related to the duties or obligations of others, whilst other rights, equally clearly, did not, being a different type of right altogether. See *Fundamental Legal Conceptions*, published in 1923. Hohfeld was primarily concerned with the precise definition of *legal* rights, but most theorists agree that although there are some differences the Hohfeldian concepts have reasonably clear parallels within *moral* rights. See, for example, Judith Jarvis Thomson, *The Realm of Rights* (1990) for a detailed interpretation.

Five - Is There a Right to Equality?

Equality is often regarded as an *ideal*. It is not always clear whether equality is considered to be an *attribute* or a *condition*, but is there a *right* to equality? Ideals and rights are very different things, of course. Ideals are often associated with aspirations and objectives which can be very different and contrary from one person to another. Rights are a different matter. However - inequality between human beings is regarded by many as *unfair* or *unjust*, so to rectify this, it is argued, there should be *rights* to equality. Let us look at this in detail. Most people would reasonably agree that *some* inequalities are unjust, but are *all* inequalities unjust?

In many cases the answer is *not always*, for example not everyone is equally eligible to do a job requiring high level skill or intelligence because not all human beings are equally skilled or intelligent. If John is more intelligent than Alan, then John is clearly at an advantage in this respect and there is an inequality. But this is not *unfair* because the advantage is based upon *natural* differences of ability between them. How can a natural difference of ability, of any sort, be *unfair* or *unjust*? As other writers have pointed out, it is not as if John has cheated in some way.

Before going any further, it is a mistake to ascribe differences in aptitude, ability etc. to differences in *education* in every case. It is perfectly true that poor education will adversely affect people's career prospects, but it is also true that some people with little or no formal education are capable of notable achievements in life whilst conversely, even with a good education some people will not do particularly well. Even the best education will not alter the fact that one person's native intelligence can be greater than another's, and the same goes for alertness, curiosity, creativity, ingenuity and so on. It is fallacious to pretend that differences in aptitude and ability are explained purely in terms of educational advantage or disadvantage in every case.

'Injustice' and 'unfairness' are words which must be used with care. If something is unjust or unfair, this means amongst other things that *someone* is accountable and blameworthy for a *wrong* that has been done or allowed to occur. Otherwise, to spell it all out, there is no injustice or unfairness. That is what those words *mean*. Therefore, if the difference between John and Alan is unjust or unfair then who, precisely, is accountable? John, perhaps? This is hardly reasonable. How can it be fair to blame him (or anyone else) for a natural difference? The 'unfairness' or 'injustice' argument very quickly collapses into confusion.

To argue that there is an injustice or an unfairness but that 'no-one is to be blamed' is merely incoherent and fails to understand the point we have just made. If no-one is blameworthy or accountable then it does not make sense to say that there is or has been a moral wrong, so there is no injustice or unfairness. The point is that not all inequalities between human beings are necessarily wrongs, in particular those that derive from natural or accidental causes.

It is sometimes argued that *because* the differences between John and Alan are natural they are 'undeserved' and are unjust on *that* basis, but this argument is fallacious. Their differences are neither 'deserved' nor 'undeserved', they are 'not deserved', which is *neutral*. This has been pointed out by many other thinkers on this question, both ancient and modern (e.g. Aristotle, Professor A.G.N. Flew). 'Undeserved' implies by definition that a *wrong* has taken place so it would follow, in these terms, that any person who is more intelligent (or stronger, or prettier, or more quick-witted etc.) than another is guilty of a 'wrong' against *every other human being* who is less intelligent, strong, pretty, quick-witted or whatever than they are. We therefore have a *reductio ad absurdum*. Similarly, although we feel sorry for Plain Jane who resents Pretty Pollyanna, Pollyanna is not guilty of an injustice against Jane or anyone else simply through being pretty. Or again, we might as well complain that the bad weather (a natural event) which we had on holiday was 'undeserved' or 'not fair'. To whom do we complain about 'natural injustice', if indeed there is such a thing? Maybe we should walk around shaking our fists up at the sky....

Some people such as the severely disabled or those with very low intelligence are *naturally* disadvantaged to a major extent, so the question arises as to how they should be *compensated*, as certain theorists put it, for their disadvantage. Clearly they are unable to work for a living or only able to do very low skill work. They need assistance with day-to-day living as well as economic support. Most people would agree that they should have some sort of compensation, for it is generally accepted that there are moral duties to avert or to alleviate natural hurts, harms or misfortunes. There are *duties of care and support* towards the less fortunate.

But (as many other thinkers have also pointed out) it is misleading to use the word 'compensate' in this particular context. A better term is 'support'. 'Compensation' ordinarily means restitution which is *owed* to people who have been *wronged by others*. But naturally occurring disadvantages are not hurts or harms that have been *inflicted* or *perpetrated* by other people. The capable and the healthy have a duty of care towards the weak and the disabled and they are *wrong* if they neglect that duty, but they did not *cause* them to be weak or disabled in the first place. *Psychologically* it is normal to feel guilty about the misfortunes of others, and this is probably what misleads some writers to 'objectify' this in terms of injustice. It would be a very sad world if we did not feel sorry for the disadvantaged, but it is not a question of 'making amends' or 'restitution' for a wrong that has been done. On the contrary, *injustice* arises if the duties of care and support are *neglected* - which is an entirely different question from 'compensation for a wrong'.

It is naive and equivocal to confuse *duties of care* towards the less *fortunate* with *restitution* for *injustice*. This is no different from overlooking the distinctions noted in Chapter Two between *moral*, *natural* and *accidental* hurts or harms. To deny or to ignore these distinctions leads to various absurdities, as we pointed out - it would be impossible to make moral distinctions between dying naturally and being murdered, between losing something and being robbed, and so on. The rights of those who are so seriously disabled that they cannot support themselves are therefore rights to care and support, not rights to 'compensation for wrongs'.

And returning to natural differences and inequalities of *ability* to do certain sorts of jobs, these may validly entail differences of income which cannot be described as unfair unless - obviously - a person's income is *so* low that they cannot afford to live (more on pay differentials very shortly). Maybe John is *very* bright whilst Alan is 'reasonably' bright, still bright enough to have a job with a reasonable albeit more modest income. It is difficult to call this a 'social injustice'.

But this must not be confused with the equality of *moral rights*. There are no natural differences between human beings that suggest any reason for not applying moral rights equally, and in Chapter Two we noted the moral wrongness of treating people *arbitrarily*. Equality of treatment is therefore a moral precept, and if 'human rights' are co-extensive in meaning with moral rights, then it follows that human rights apply equally to all human beings. This rules out discrimination between human beings for reasons such as ethnicity, gender, creed, class, disability or age. In the field of employment, therefore, *equality of treatment* means that there should be *equal opportunities*. Thus it is morally *invalid* to refuse to employ someone on grounds of ethnicity, gender etc.. It is *valid*, however, to apply *relevant* criteria such as the skills, qualifications or prior experience required to do a job, and this is not the same as treating people arbitrarily or applying invalid or irrelevant criteria.

Also, although there is a moral right to *equality of treatment*, this is not the same as *substantive* equality in terms of income, where it is possible to justify *fair inequality*. As we noted in Chapter One, if your job is more complex, demanding and responsible than another less onerous job, many would consider you have a right to be paid more. And if fairness means anything at all, it is *unfair* if you are both paid the same. Incentives *to* work and rewards *for* work are also morally valid for the pursuit of achievement and excellence. Consider too all the difficult, demanding, dangerous and disagreeable jobs which would not get done without special recompense.

We therefore identify the *demands* a job makes upon the jobholder as being *morally relevant criteria* for a pay differential. Arguably, any system of remuneration and reward that overlooks this key element is inherently *unjust*. This is why it is *unfair* if the job you do is paid the same as another job which is less demanding than yours.

In this connection, job evaluation and performance related pay schemes as used in many large organizations show how pay differentials can be fairly based upon objective criteria consistently applied. Jobs can be graded according to set criteria such as level of skill or qualifications required, scope of responsibility, decisions required, consequences of error, work complexity, special conditions and so on, forming the basis of an equitable system of pay differentials. On a point of detail, note that the *job*, not the person doing it, is graded. This is done on the basis of a job description which summarizes the duties and responsibilities, with no reference to the jobholder's identity, sex, age etc. Also, job evaluation is capable of assessing how *wide* or *narrow* the differential should be between one job and another. But the important point is that insofar as jobs are evaluated according to the same criteria, there is *equality of treatment*.

Job evaluation is a suitable paradigm for any sort of *fairness* which we can define as *the determination of morally valid equivalences, differences or differentials by relevant and consistent criteria.* But this is not the same as equality of *result* or of *outcome*. People claim 'equal pay for equal work', not 'equal pay' pure and simple (and by parity of reasoning, 'equal pay for equal work' implies 'unequal pay for unequal work'). Comparably, equality before the law does not mean that all accused persons should be found equally innocent (or, for that matter, equally guilty). It means equality of treatment *by relevant and consistent criteria.*

The 'even Stevens' concept of equality has largely been abandoned when it comes to pay. The first Soviet government found it necessary as early as 1918 to restore pay differentials between skilled and unskilled workers. British trade unionists have always been concerned to maintain pay differentials related to skill. Most women accept that *if* Steven does a more complex and demanding job than Stephanie, then it is right that he should be paid more - provided that if Stephanie does a more complex and demanding job than Steven, then she should be paid more.   If they are doing the same job or different but comparable jobs as determined by job evaluation, then the basic pay should be the same.   If surveys show that women are consistently paid less than men for *comparable jobs*, then women are justified in complaining, particularly if equal pay legislation has been on the Statute Book since 1970.

On the other hand a pay differential could still be justified in a particular situation if one person consistently and demonstrably produces greater output than another.   Maybe Ben works harder or more intelligently than Bill, shows more initiative, makes fewer mistakes, and so on.   Or maybe Steven, for example, frequently takes periods of time off work for one reason or another.   Whether there are good reasons for his absences or not, it is not unfair in the circumstances that Stephanie should be paid more and considered more eligible for promotion.   This is particularly relevant in managerial jobs - while Steven is away, Stephanie continues to accumulate the greater knowledge and experience which is necessary for career advancement and which also justifies a higher salary.   But this is not taking unfair advantage; she is not playing office politics, for example.   No 'wrong' has taken place.   It is not unfair that after a few years have passed Stephanie ends up in senior management while Steven is still in middle management.   He may not like it, but he has no grounds for complaint.

Now suppose it is Stephanie who takes periods of time off work, to have children from time to time.

Of course, the reason for Stephanie's absence is different from Steven's, but the *category* of reason is the same - an employee's absence from work (or resignation) for reasons *of their own* as distinct from reasons which are at the employer's instigation (e.g. suspension, lay-off, etc.). So it is Stephen who begins to accumulate the greater experience which is necessary for promotion to a more senior job. But this is not an unfair advantage for no wrong has taken place.

Pregnancy and child rearing are probably an important reason why, after decades of legislation, the figures compiled in various surveys show that there are still fewer women than men in the most senior positions in industry, commerce and in the professions. No doubt in some cases this is still because of *discrimination*, but is this the only explanation in every case? An alternative explanation for them is also possible: namely, career interruption resulting from pregnancy. The question of which explanation applies is not, of course, a matter of rights or of ethics, it is a methodological question. But the figures in themselves do not provide an answer.

As in other contexts, moral blame cannot be imputed to differences between different people's circumstances or situations which ultimately originate from natural causes. In Stephanie's case, the causal factor is pregnancy and child rearing. 'Positive discrimination' legislation to increase the 'quota' of women in the most senior positions may in part be based upon flawed reasoning, namely that a wrong needs to be rectified. But it has not been shown that this is always the case, and it should also be noted that if it is unjust to refuse promotion to a woman because she is a woman then it is also unjust, under positive discrimination, to refuse promotion to a man because he is a man.

Men and women both have equal moral rights. But neither have rights to the rectification of wrongs that have not taken place, and as we have said, discrimination is not necessarily the only explanation for gender inequality. There are, of course, laws and political objectives to increase the ratio of women in senior positions. It is well known that when women reach high positions in various fields - science, law, politics etc. - they usually excel. It is therefore in the interests of society as a whole that there should be more women in senior positions. But this, also, is not a question of rights to the rectification of wrongs. And once again, we emphasize that in this and in many of the preceding paragraphs, we are only reiterating what many other thinkers have said before.

But other difficult questions remain. Job evaluation schemes tend only to apply to differentials within a specific organization; job evaluation has nothing to do with the fact that, for example, company A in the chemical industry sets higher pay levels than company B in engineering. Likewise the private sector usually pays more, job for job, than the public sector (although the latter usually offers better job security). Most people accept that unusually demanding and responsible jobs such as managing directors, prime ministers etc. should be paid considerably more than most other jobs, and the contribution made by successful business entrepreneurs to the economy and society generally is well known. They have a right to their high earnings. On the other hand, is it right that footballers and entertainers should earn more in a week than doctors, nurses and teachers earn in a year?

This is a complex and debatable question. Other things being equal, doctors, nurses and teachers can reasonably expect secure, gainful employment until they are well into their sixties. This is not the case with sports people. And it has always been true that although some actors (for example) become rich and famous, the overwhelming majority only obtain irregular, 'as and when' employment, living in many cases in very modest circumstances. This suggests a high risk/high reward concept of remuneration which has its own rationale. Perhaps it is not so unreasonable after all.

Yet another question concerns Joe Soap who wins the lottery, becoming more wealthy overnight than most other people. Most people would wish him well, but certain people would regard his good fortune as arbitrary and therefore *unfair*. But he paid for his lottery ticket like millions of other people, and how can it be wrong to be *lucky*? Or *unlucky*? One man lives to be 95 whilst another drops dead of a heart attack at 39. This is sad, but it is not a *wrong*. Otherwise we might just as well argue that women's longer lifespans than men's are unfair, unjust, undeserved etc. etc. and, as such, are contrary to men's equality rights for which there should be 'restitution' etc. etc..... Or again, if a motor insurance company offers preferential premiums to women because they have fewer accidents and convictions than men, this is, literally, 'sex discrimination' but it is *for a valid reason.* It is absurd and dogmatic to say that it infringes men's rights to equality, and there is no moral or logical incongruity.

Six - Dilemmas and Other Problems

Privacy might be considered a good example of a right which cannot be validly overridden by any other rights, duties or actions of other people. Physical privacy in the bedroom and the bathroom is an obvious example under normal circumstances. But under not so normal circumstances, if perhaps you are a dangerous criminal on the run, the police might consider they have an overriding duty to interrupt your slumbers. Or if you are robbing a bank, the CCTV camera is not an 'invasion of your privacy rights'. Even if it is, other considerations happen to be more important.

Take a couple of other examples. Suppose you don't show up for work one day. Your employer has a valid claim-right that you should be there and she might reasonably consider herself within her rights to phone you if she still hasn't heard from you by the afternoon. This is a reasonable interruption of your privacy. Ditto for the *duty* (and therefore the *right*) of the police to interview you, urgently, if you're a witness or a suspect in a murder enquiry (or, indeed, any other).

In many cases, therefore, the right to privacy is conditional, dependent upon circumstances. But other types of privacy are stronger. Medical records and bank account details are strictly private to the individual and *only* to those others who have legitimate access to that information such as medical staff, bank staff and so on. Anyone without authorization has no morally valid access to personal information about you, with a clear duty not to access that information. So you have a right to privacy in a much fuller and more comprehensive sense than in the other examples. Thanks to the Internet there are major concerns about unauthorized access to personal information, hackers, identity theft, staff carelessness and management incompetence. Modern computers now make it possible to lose not just a few files but the equivalent of thousands of filing cabinets all at once.

Consider another kind of privacy. Some people query the right of the media to invade the personal privacy of famous people 'in the public interest'. Media freedom, of course, is a *liberty right*, but liberty rights are always *conditional*, only valid so long as there is *no duty not* to do something. But everyone has a *duty not* to gratuitously cause embarrassment or annoyance to other people, famous or otherwise, these being more serious hurts or harms than denials of Joe Public's appetite for gratuitous gossip or tittle-tattle. And critics could also query what right does anyone have to know the ins and outs of other people's lives outside of their own circle?

On the other hand, although the 'public interest' argument is often over-used by apologists for the media it *is* in the public interest to publicize for example the activities of a Cabinet Minister who is taking bribes, something the public would have a very definite right to know about. And media freedom to criticize governments and politicians is a very important part of the political process in a free society.

Yet another issue concerns closed circuit TV cameras in public places. Are they not a threat to our personal privacy and, as such, a breach of our civil liberties? Others might disagree, arguing that the whole object of CCTV cameras is to protect public safety, to safeguard people's more fundamental rights not to be attacked or hindered in public places. So long as you are not up to no good yourself you have nothing to fear. And if these cameras are got rid of, wouldn't that undermine our other civil liberties to go about our lawful business without let or hindrance? There can be prolonged debates on this question.

Is there a right to be told the truth?
We could respond to this question with another one - 'who has the right to know?'. People always have a *need to know* about matters that have a bearing on their lives, welfare, concerns and interests, hence the Freedom of Information Act. Also, to knowingly make false statements is potentially and usually harmful to people. It is therefore recognized in all moral codes that that lying and deceit are serious moral wrongs, and it follows that there are moral rights not to be lied to or deceived. There are 'negative' claim-rights not to be lied to or deceived, as well as 'positive' claim-rights to be told the truth. But these do not necessarily mean the same thing and people sometimes confuse the two.

This is because there are interesting exceptions to the duty to tell the truth. It has often been pointed out that tact, discretion and diplomacy also have a moral basis, restraining us from being over-frank with people in ways they might find embarrassing or upsetting. And a well known character in many large organizations is the senior executive (or politician) who disdains advice which he or she has no wish to know about, so that underlings often have duties *not* to tell the truth. They can face difficult dilemmas. Again, in negotiating situations you might be under strict instructions from your employer (or client) not to divulge information about actual or possible future plans, either to competitors or to anyone else. Other parties have rights not to be lied to and that material facts should not be withheld, but this is not the same as having a right to be told anything and everything. In many situations you can have legitimate duties (and therefore rights) to be less than open about things.

And there can be other duties *not* to tell the truth. Doctors, priests, teachers, psychiatrists, social workers, bank managers and many others are privy to sensitive and confidential information they are duty-bound to reveal to no-one. It should be noted, of course, that because their duties are valid, they also have *rights* not to divulge the truth to anyone who lacks a legitimate right to know. It follows that the right to be told the truth can have limitations for valid reasons, which is why it is not the same as the negative right not to be lied to or deceived.

Difficult situations can arise, of course. If the police are conducting a murder enquiry and believe their suspect's priest, doctor, psychiatrist or whoever has information which is materially relevant, they could say their right to be told the truth should not have the same limitations that apply to other people. There can be differences of view on this question. Serious dilemmas can arise too. Jill assures Jack that she can always keep a secret, come what may, but if he tells her that he once murdered someone and was never caught, she realizes to her dismay that that's *different*. What should she do....? The police and many other people have a *right to know* about what happened.

Another complex and seemingly paradoxical issue is that governments and the security services have overriding duties to protect your safety and your interests through adequate security measures. Often this means secrecy, so you may have no right to know about certain things although this is *really* in your own best interests. Governments have overriding duties to safeguard national security, and as we have already noted, if you have a valid duty to do something then you have a right to do it.

The right to life is often believed to be based upon the precept that 'life is the most fundamental value of all'. But the problem is that *values* are relative from one culture to another, even from one person to another. So the question shifts back to how do we justify one value or another one? As pointed out in Chapter Two, we need a criterion *which is not itself a value*. And the relativism of value is very different from the absolute value of life which some people believe in. Also, if we value 'life' as a generality, what sense does it make to value the lives of viruses, cancer cells or disease-carrying pests such as rats? If we *don't* value those life-forms - which is reasonable enough - then what *criterion* enables us to determine which life-forms should be valued and which should not be?

Some people suggest that the most complex life-forms are the most valuable, but why does complexity *as such* necessarily possess value? Jennifer's cat is less complex than a human being, but she'd want to say that her cat's life is of immense value. Adolf Hitler was a highly complex living creature, but human or not, did his life possess value at all? This is a very debatable question, but the mere fact that it is debatable suggests that it is far from 'self-evident'.

But even if something does possess 'value', we would presumably wish to say that we *must* value it, but how do we infer *obligation* from a value? As a matter of pure logic the one does not follow from the other. Another point is that we know that rights and obligations are correlatives, so if there is a right to life there must presumably be a correlative obligation (somewhere) such as the obligation to respect life. But how does that *follow from* a value? A value is only a preference, after all. Nothing possesses 'objective' or intrinsic value; to say that something is valuable is only to say that 'it is valued' by somebody. So the basic question remains - where does the obligation to respect life come from?

We suggest that respecting life is not a value or an article of faith, it is *implied* as a moral concept. The core moral precept is the starting point, stipulating the requirement to respect others as well as yourself. But fairly obviously, it is the principal *necessary condition*, or *implicit presupposition*, of respecting others that they should be *alive*. It follows that respecting the lives of others is the very *first* obligation and the right to life follows from that as a correlative. The right to life is therefore the *primary* human right. In these terms the right to life is not a question of value, it is an obligation. 'Intrinsic value' concepts are therefore unnecessary.

But many difficult questions remain. Are we obliged to respect *all* lives? Do all living creatures have a right to life? Is the right to life absolute? Interpreted as the right *not to be killed* (i.e. as a negative claim-right), the right to life is a morally overriding right but in the most *extreme* circumstances it can be forfeited. If you violently attack another person in such a way as to give them reason to believe that their life is in danger, that person has a right to self-defence which is also based on the right to life. If, in a desperate situation, they are forced to fight back and you get killed as a result, that is your own fault, not theirs. How can they be blamed for defending themselves? If we deny a person's right to effective self-defence, then in practical terms we have denied the right to life of an innocent party. No theory of rights or ethics with this result can be considered viable. Interestingly, however, *laws* on the right to self-defence vary from one country to another.

Another example - a homicidal maniac is shooting at random into a playground full of children and is shot dead by an armed policeman. But this is not a violation of his right to life because he forfeited it himself. There are also other issues with the right to life. Although the right to life implies the right not to be killed, it is important not to confuse the right not to be killed with the *right not to be murdered*, although many people do confuse the two.   By definition, you can never be murdered 'by accident', it is always deliberate and with malice aforethought.   But you can be killed by accident where no-one is to blame, as in certain sorts of road accidents.   Not all of them result from dangerous driving or other sorts of culpable negligence; a driver cannot be blamed for a lapse in concentration if he is stung by a wasp, for example. Life can sometimes be lost through force of circumstances which are nobody's fault and which are not, therefore, a culpable infringement of rights.

The other complication is that life cannot be sustained without food, fuel, shelter and other services and benefits such as medical care.   But these constitute positive claim-rights which can be limited through force of circumstances, and defaults on obligations can sometimes be blameless, as we have seen.   Life is often contingent upon circumstances which rights cannot always change. People sometimes say that their right to medical care is directly based upon their right to life, so that if their right to life must not be infringed, then their right to medical care must not be infringed.

But sadly, this is only half-true and conflates two separate issues.   The two rights may converge, but they do not mean the *same* and the former cannot entail the latter because your right to medical care can be limited, through nobody's fault, by lack of resources.   It costs billions of pounds to research, develop and test certain specialized drugs and medications which is why they cost so much. They cannot all be provided free otherwise the NHS would have no money left over for anything else. The right to life cannot alter that.

Is there a right to abortion?   On a point of definition, any termination of a life is 'killing', strictly speaking.   Therefore if we terminate the life of a foetus, we are killing it.   But killing can sometimes be morally permissible (as in self-defence in a perilous situation), sometimes not (as in murder).   So, is abortion morally permissible or otherwise?   In these terms, abortion is most obviously justified when it is for medical reasons and the life of the mother is in danger.

The most contentious issue is abortion for *non-medical* reasons.   This question is frequently debated in terms of rights, either the mother's rights, the unborn child's rights or even, in some cases, the rights of the father.   But we shall not consider rights just yet.   A more fundamental question than rights is whether something is *the right thing to do*, or not.   If having an abortion is morally permissible then clearly, it makes no sense to dispute whether a woman has a right to it.   On the other hand, if having an abortion is wrong then, equally clearly, the question of rights does not arise. We therefore address the ethics of abortion to begin with.

Consider a pro-abortion argument first of all. Many would say that a lot depends on the stage of development the foetus is *at*.   If abortion takes place within the first few weeks of conception (say), it is not really a living creature 'in its own right'. It is *part of* its mother's body, not a distinct entity, and mothers like anyone else have prerogative rights over their own bodies which no-one else has. It only makes sense to kill a life that is separate from your own (unless, perhaps, you are committing suicide), so abortion cannot therefore count as 'killing'. It could also be argued that the foetus is not *self-sustaining* or *viable* as an independent being, as a different living entity, because it depends upon the mother for everything. It is *part of* the mother, in that sense, and this is sometimes called the *viability argument*.

Now consider an anti-abortion argument. It could be agreed that everyone has rights over their own bodies which no-one else has, and it does sound odd to talk of 'killing' what is part of your own body. But the foetus is not 'part of' the mother's body. It is within the mother's body, attached to it and fully dependent on it, but from the instant of conception it is a distinct living entity in its own right. It is *genetically distinct* because the DNA is different, as unique to each individual as a fingerprint. The foetus has a separate *identity*, and 'connected to' does not always or necessarily mean the same as 'part of'. If it were really 'part of' the mother's body, the DNA would be the same. This refutes the 'part of my body' argument. Of course, the earlier pro-abortionists (1960's) could not have been aware of DNA's implications.

Because the foetus is a distinctly identifiable living entity the mother does not have rights over it, she has obligations towards it. This is particularly the case if it is not self-sustaining, so that the viability argument rebounds upon itself - all the more reason for caring for it, not killing it. It is 'her' foetus, true, but it is not a possession to be discarded at will any more than a child is. Abortion for non-medical reasons is killing in the most literal meaning of the word, completely different from abortion for medical reasons or miscarriage. Nor is it accidental killing, for abortions are not carried out by accident. It is deliberate killing which is therefore murder.

The pro-abortionist might regard this line of reasoning as an overstatement. One may accept that strictly speaking the foetus is a distinct entity in its own right and that abortion is - strictly speaking - killing. But if it is only at very early stage of development (say a week or so), it is implausible to call this *murder*. There is a right to life, but is this not a matter of *degree*? How can it be murder to kill a tiny entity that has hardly developed its own nervous system? It is hardly a human being at all. And the pro-abortionist might hope it is not being suggested that aborting a week old foetus should entail life imprisonment for murder.

This is a debate which could go on for a considerable time. Is there, however, a means of unlocking the deadlock between each side? We can probably agree that it is implausible to call abortion *murder* in the very early stages of pregnancy. Although the DNA is unique, the foetus is not yet a *human being* any more than a seed is a flower - *yet*. In this sense, at the earlier stages of pregnancy, the ethical objections to abortion are difficult to sustain. But a few months on, the foetus has begun to acquire some clear indications of 'human-ness' - a face, a brain, a nervous system, the ability to feel pain, and so on. Here, as others have suggested, a concept of unethical killing sounds more plausible, though many would still be reluctant to call this *murder*.

Now, there is no immediately obvious point where the line should be drawn between the opposite ends of the spectrum. We cannot say it is definitely permissible to abort up to a precise point in time but unethical killing the following *day*, any more than we can pinpoint an exact moment when day ceases to be day and becomes night. But it is clear that a line must be drawn *somewhere*, and this could be done according to a specific criterion for example the ability to feel *pain*.

A woman's reasons for wanting an abortion will also have a bearing on whether having an abortion is ethical or not. Pregnancy resulting from rape should make abortion permissible, fairly obviously. If the foetus has serious abnormalities, it cannot be right to bring a lifetime of major suffering into the world. It is also true that unwanted pregnancies bring severe and increased hardship to mothers who are already struggling against poverty. But if abortion is only for reasons of convenience there is room for moral doubt, even at a fairly early stage of pregnancy.

Now let us turn to rights. What if restricting abortion denies the rights of women? This is true, but inconclusive. It is equally true that the laws against slander are contrary to my right to free speech, but there are very good reasons for those laws, more important than 'my rights'. Like many other issues, abortion is much too complex a question to be analysed - let alone resolved - purely in terms of rights.

A complicating factor is that as well as resolutely pro-abortion feminists there are also anti-abortion feminists. They say that abortion is an act of violence, something it pleases women to condemn men for. And it is invidious for women to proclaim a feminist ethic of caring whilst showing little care for their own unborn children. Another point is that if abortion is a right it would be a *liberty right*, but liberty rights are *conditional*. All human beings are subject to the obligation not to kill, and rights do not just mean you are free to do whatever you like or to make up your own moral rules at will (betraying, perhaps, a radical misconception of what rights are all about). This is why many have said that abortion is not just a women's issue, the implications are much wider.

Ironically, two of the most cogent arguments for abortion have no direct connection with 'women's rights' as such. Firstly, abortion is an obvious method of reducing the very major evils which result from over-population. Secondly, stem-cell research shows clear indications of achieving major breakthroughs in the treatment of a variety of serious diseases affecting millions of people. Providing abortion takes place *early*, it is difficult to sustain ethical objections to these considerations.

Euthanasia There are different *types* of euthanasia. The main distinctions are between *voluntary* euthanasia, *involuntary* euthanasia and *non-voluntary* euthanasia. These are clearly summarized by Jonathan Glover in *Causing Death and Saving Lives*, 1977. *Voluntary* euthanasia is where, as a result of your own expressed wishes, doctors put you to death or allow you to die because you have *chosen* to die, maybe through a 'living will' written in the past. Sometimes this is called 'assisted suicide'. Maybe you are suffering from an incurable and painful disease and because it is *at your own explicit wish* that your life is terminated, many regard this as a form of mercy killing which is completely different from *murder*.

Then there is *involuntary* and *non-voluntary* euthanasia. Involuntary euthanasia is where a person is put to death, ostensibly in their own best interests, but disregarding or not seeking to ascertain their wishes. Most people would agree that this would be unethical and criminal killing - deliberate murder and not, therefore, to be considered any further. Non-voluntary euthanasia is where although no wish to die has been expressed or recorded, a person *cannot express* their wishes. So in the case of *involuntary* euthanasia there are those who maybe *can* express a wish but *haven't*, but with *non-voluntary* euthanasia they have not expressed a wish to die because they *cannot*. It is useful to consider the different types of euthanasia in turn.

Apart from being 'brain dead' where a person's body is artificially kept alive in a vegetative state through machinery, most people's main concerns revolve around those 'grey areas' where a wish to die has not been expressed. What if someone is semi-conscious and unable to express his wishes? There is reason to believe he is in pain and uncomfortable. He may be *dying* but he is still *alive*. Should his relatives be allowed, legally and morally, to request the doctors to terminate his life if there is no prospect of any recovery? Or would that be murder pure and simple?   Suppose there is room for reasonable doubt as to whether he would *wish* to die?

This is arguably murder pure and simple, for the obvious reason that you cannot make the assumption that he wishes to die.   Another problem with borderline cases is that even if he can communicate, indirect pressure could be brought to bear upon him, done very subtly, of course, to express a willingness to die.   This could be called 'constructive murder'.   It could come from the relatives, or anyone.   Even to make a suggestion would be a form of pressure too.

We can reasonably accept in 'grey area' cases that it is murder to bring about death through deliberate actions such as lethal injections.   This is often called *direct* euthanasia and it is very difficult to maintain that *direct* euthanasia, non-voluntary as well as involuntary, is anything other than murder. But *indirect* non-voluntary euthanasia may be different if a patient is *allowed to die* through discontinuing medical treatment.   The idea is that we 'let nature take its course' if it is *certain* that cure or recovery is impossible, and medically certified as such.   What if the doctors are agreed that a patient's condition is hopeless?

Suppose the only thing the doctors can do is not to cure, which is no longer possible, but only to relieve pain, often only at the cost of making the patient unconscious?   Is it not a mercy to end suffering? This argument is very cogent in relation to *non-voluntary* euthanasia.   However, some would argue that there is only a fine distinction between directly ending life and indirectly allowing to die, and others would argue that there is no real distinction at all. The reader should give very careful thought to this question.

Concluding with *voluntary* euthanasia, many argue that if a person has expressed a *wish* to die this is completely different from the other types of euthanasia. What if someone says 'it *is* in my best interests that I be put to death - please do so'? It is a basic moral rule that we should seek to reduce suffering, not to prolong it, which is a very compelling obligation. Arguably, it would be cruel not to respect the wishes of a person in pain. Do they not have, in this sense, a right to die? The right to life is implied by the very concept of ethics as a matter of principle, but if the right-holder *does not want* that right anymore then aren't people relieved of their obligation to keep them alive? In other circumstances we are normally relieved of our obligations to others if they are declined for one reason or another. In this case, is it not only a difference of degree?

Crime and Punishment   With the exception of people misclassified as criminals (e.g. prostitutes and various others), many criminals deliberately abuse the rights of other human beings, sometimes very seriously. This makes them a particularly interesting group of human beings. In this section we shall concentrate on various issues concerning their *rights* and their *responsibility*. For example, is imprisonment an infringement of the 'basic human right to freedom'? The short answer is that it is more accurately described as a *curtailment* of freedom in order to protect the rights of *other* *people* which is a valid and overriding consideration, as we have noted before. To take the most obvious example, no society can allow serial killers etc. to be left at liberty. Public safety comes first.

Of course, public safety is not the only consideration when dealing with criminals. Serious offenders still have to be punished even if, in some cases, they are not, or are no longer, a danger to others. As is often said, 'justice must not only be done, it must be seen to be done'. Related to this, punishment is also for the purpose of deterring *potential* offenders. But a principal purpose of punishment is to make it clear to the offender that society disapproves of the offence and takes it seriously - otherwise, why should the offender take it seriously? It is sometimes suggested that this does not work in practice because the proportion of those who re-offend after punishment is very high, but in view of the fact that prison sentences have been getting progressively shorter over the past few decades, this is not surprising.

However, even though it is necessary to lock people up for one reason or another, it does not follow that society is entitled to withdraw certain other rights from offenders. They still have rights to justice and to fairness, to food, clothing, medical care etc. and the right not to be subjected to 'cruel and unusual' punishments. With proper guidance, delinquent individuals can often be rehabilitated into society successfully and this is particularly the case with young offenders. It is absurd to lock people up and 'throw away the key'.

On the other hand, this does not mean that because an offender has rights, there is a 'right not to be punished'. Punishment is seen by some people as a 'wrong' which society inflicts upon offenders (*see* the left-wing press), but it is only a *wrong* if the punishment is inhumane, disproportionate to the offence or fails to make due allowance for genuinely mitigating circumstances. If punishment is said to be wrong as a matter of principle simply because it is 'hurtful' to a greater or lesser extent, then we cannot even have speeding fines.

Nor does having rights mean that criminals (or anyone else) are not culpable for their own actions. Unless you have been forced to do something against your will or genuinely accidentally, you act of your own volition, so that you personally are *liable*. This is as true of a criminal act as of any other. Therefore when society rescinds an offender's right to freedom, he has forfeited it himself because of the action(s) *he* chose to do. The point of principle is that if someone has forfeited their own rights it makes no sense to say that someone else, or society, has infringed them. Further, you can still be responsible and liable even if you haven't acted deliberately or intentionally at all. You did not intend to kill the child you ran over, but if you were using your mobile phone, for example, you were *culpably negligent*.

It is true that a fair criminal justice system should take account of an offender's deprived upbringing or other factors such as economic deprivation. There can also be mitigating circumstances, for example a woman who has suffered violence and abuse from her husband for many years but 'snaps' one day and kills him with the carving knife. But many criminals and anti-social individuals have never suffered deprivation or mitigating circumstances at all. Al Capone for example came from a good family background. So it is hazardous to generalize, to construct blanket hypotheses on the causes of crime or to ignore the issue of individual responsibility altogether. Correlations between crime and economic deprivation do not always or necessarily denote *causality*, nor do they always excuse particular actions.

For, even if an individual has been deprived and cannot help the way he was brought up, it does not follow that he *cannot help* his own actions or that he has no responsibility for them (unless there are special circumstances as with a *crime passionel*). *Very few* human beings literally cannot help what they are doing, and if you can help what you are doing you are accountable for it and liable.

Conversely, if a person *literally* and *genuinely* cannot help his own actions e.g. through mental illness or incapacity, you would still have (even more so, in fact) a very dangerous individual at large. Whether you're 'bad' or 'sad', you've still got to be locked up, one way or another, if you're a danger to others, with the proviso that in the case of the 'sad', treatment should be included. The same could reasonably apply to those with a propensity to commit dangerous or criminally irresponsible acts whilst under the influence of drink or drugs. Public safety still comes first.

However, the 'no responsibility' argument persists, for all criminals and for crime in general. It is still said that because of their upbringing, background, socially conditioned behavioural dispositions, genetic factors etc., criminals can't help being criminals. But if we take this literally, you might as well argue that for exactly the same reasons none of us can help being as we are, therefore none of us can be held responsible, for anything. But where would that leave 'rights'? Remembering that the whole idea of 'rights' presupposes that other people have a *responsibility* towards you against which you make claims and so on, if the concept of responsibility is vacuous then so, necessarily, is the concept of 'rights' - for anyone. If no-one is responsible, then nobody has rights, neither criminals nor anyone else.

The same issue arises with the *fallacy of misplaced responsibility*. It may be true that Jason's upbringing was less than perfect for all sorts of reasons. Or maybe his parents were foolish in letting him 'set his own rules' out of a misguided 'respect for his rights'. But it does not follow that we should always shift the blame to other people (or to society) as a matter of principle. For, why stop there? In exactly the same way we should blame *other people's* faults and failings upon 'other people' in turn and so on *ad infinitum*. In the end we cannot rationally hold anyone to account for anything, in which case, as before, the entire notion of responsibility *and of rights* collapses. And the difficulty is, of course, that those who proclaim one version or another of the 'no responsibility' thesis also want to insist that Jason 'has rights'. But this is impossible if the 'no responsibility' thesis is taken to its logical conclusion.

There is another unexpected implication of the 'no responsibility' thesis which gives us yet another *reductio ad absurdum*. We would ordinarily wish to condemn the officials of a police state which tortures political prisoners, but we cannot rationally condemn the officials or the torturers if, just like Jason, they cannot help their upbringing, background, behavioural dispositions etc. and should also, therefore, be excused of responsibility for their actions and exempted from punishment. This would be a very disagreeable conclusion to human rights fundamentalists, the 'politically correct' *et alia*, but it follows from the 'no responsibility' thesis as surely as night follows day. Unless you are arbitrarily adopting a 'pick and mix' approach, it does not make sense to apply one theory of mind and behaviour (free will and responsibility) to those you don't like, or disapprove of, and another set of presuppositions (non-responsibility) in the case of those you favour or feel sorry for. To put it another way, the 'no responsibility' thesis only backfires on you.

Finally we must consider the *resources* required to look after criminals who end up in prison. Most people would agree that they should receive reasonable food, medical care, clothing, heating, lighting etc. and there should also be *counselling* and *rehabilitation*. These last items are of particular interest since victims of crime could argue that they have a *comparable claim* on this particular resource, especially for care and support after they have been robbed or attacked or after a close relative has been murdered. In a book on rights, the rights of crime victims are a pertinent consideration when discussing crime and punishment.

The ticking bomb The "core moral precept", Chapter Two, defined wrongness as hurting or harming others with a scale of seriousness ranging from the minimal to the severe. The right not to be tortured is therefore a morally overriding right as are the rights not to be murdered, raped, attacked and so on. There would appear to be no circumstances where it can be morally valid to torture another human being - but consider a possible counter-example.

Suppose the security services of a country believe it is necessary to torture a captured spy or terrorist in order to obtain vitally important information which is required *urgently*. Suppose that without this information a radiological bomb will be exploded in a large city *tomorrow*. The national Head of Security might argue that unless this information is obtained *right now*, the lives of tens of thousands of people will be endangered and torture is the only way to obtain this information. Also suppose that conventional interrogation only meets with silence.

In moral terms it should be remembered that hurt or harm to others cannot be excluded when it is necessary for self-defence. It is morally right to fight defensive wars, it is morally permissible to hit back if you are attacked, otherwise there is no right of self-defence. Can this proviso, or something like it, apply to torture in the circumstances we have just outlined?

Some would say it is invalid to compare torturing the prisoner to fighting defensive wars that *have* to be fought, or fighting back against violent attack that *has* to be resisted. Those are *no-choice* situations, but there is always the choice *not* to torture, particularly when the feared terrorist outrage has not taken place *yet*. Secondly, even when defensive wars have to be fought, there is no excuse for committing war-crimes and it could be argued that war-crimes and torture fall into the same moral category. Thirdly, if the Head of Security decides not to authorize torture but the bomb explodes, who is responsible for that? The terrorists are, not the Head of Security. Accordingly the Head of Security cannot be held accountable if the outrage takes place. And since torture is among the *most* evil of acts, then anyone who authorizes or practices it is no longer a 'moral agent'.

However - the Head of Security could disagree that he has a *choice* not to do whatever is necessary when the lives of tens of thousands of people are at stake. On the contrary, he might say it is a genuine *no-choice* situation. It is misleading to say that the terrorist outrage has not taken place 'yet' when there is every reason to believe that it *will*. Nor is it valid to argue that if the bomb goes off, the Head of Security is blameless because the terrorists are responsible. For he could say, "if I fail to take *every* means within my power to prevent a disaster, then I am accountable *too*. And a principle or law which forces me to give a higher priority to the rights of one person (hardly an innocent party, either) as against the rights of thousands is morally *false*, and *that* is what would negate any claim I have to be a moral agent."

It could be pointed out that in extremely urgent and exceptional circumstances, as per the ticking bomb, torture *is* an act of valid defence of the lives of tens of thousands of people. This is very different from the use of torture in situations that are not *immediately urgent*. But a different Head of Security might argue that "torture is the most evil of acts so that *irrespective* of the circumstances or consequences, I can never condone, approve or authorize the torture of another human being. Like murder or unprovoked violent attack, it can never have *any* moral justification. Killing can be justified in exceptional cases of *self-defence*, but deliberate torture never has *any* justification." Maybe 'truth drugs' such as sodium pentothal are the only answer, and the debate continues.

Relativism Rights *vary*, sometimes markedly, from one society to another and from one historical period to another. This supports the *relativist* thesis that far from being fundamental, universal and objectively valid, rights are as relative as the values, conventions, *mores* and belief systems within which they are supposedly rooted.

All theories of rights and of ethics must address relativism, a complex issue which needs to be properly understood. Confusingly, its factual basis is open to interpretation so that different conclusions are drawn from it which are sometimes false. Equally confusingly, relativists come in different shapes and sizes. The more thorough-going relativists will include human rights within the scope of relativism and will assert that human rights are as relative as anything else. Others will proclaim their relativism to show how trendy they are, but will still insist on human rights. This is inconsistent, of course - if you believe in fundamental, universal human rights, you are not a relativist.

For our present purposes, we shall make the working assumption that we are dealing with the more thorough-going relativist who argues that there are no fundamental universal moral truths at all nor, therefore, any universal human rights at all. The relativist would argue that if *all* human beings have a set of specific, universal human rights such as the rights to life, liberty, free speech and so on, in theory we should expect to find that all human societies would uniformly recognize these rights, irrespective of special declarations about them. The trouble is, they do not. There is also a large number of human rights which only make sense in modern times and which would have been strange, outrageous or simply meaningless in past ages. For example we could mention the rights of women to equal career opportunities with men, the right to worship in the religion of one's choice, the right to openly criticize monarchs and/or elected leaders, the right to publish or broadcast more or less whatever you like, the right to go on strike, the right to vote in elections, to name but a few. The right to personal liberty is the most notable one of all, of course.

But the foregoing is not such a cogent argument as it might first appear to be. The non-relativist, or 'objectivist', could argue yes, *of course* there have been long term changes in social norms and so on, but this is only because society itself has changed. None of this obviates the fact that certain basic rights are *timeless* such as the rights to live, to eat, to procreate, to be respected, to be told the truth and so on.

The objectivist could argue that without these basic rights no society is possible at all, and the relativist cannot deny the existence of a set of *basic* rights any more than he can deny the almost universal necessity for most human beings to be clothed and housed for protection against the elements. The fact that styles of clothing are somewhat different as between 2000 BC and 2000 AD is beside the point. Also, the relativist cannot deny that upon closer inspection, any human society of whatever sort needs laws and generally accepted notions of 'right' and 'wrong' of *some* sort in order to function *as* a society. There are no known exceptions to this, even with highly diversified modern societies which have their own subcultures of one sort or another.

In appraising relativism, interpretation difficulties often arise because some relativists emphasize the dissimilarities between different societies and cultures whilst others highlight the similarities. When the similarities are studied more carefully, it will be seen that there *is* a universal set of norms to be found in all cultures and societies.

For example, all human societies, past and present, East and West, from the most primitive to the most modern, regard as murder as wrong (always distinguished from the rightness of killing, if necessary, an enemy who has attacked you).

There is a universal concept of the rightness of caring for children and the duty of ensuring their safety and well-being.   This, together with the concept of culpable murder, suggests respecting human lives.   Similarly, rape, gross cruelty and deception are universally regarded as serious wrongs, implying respect for human persons, their safety and their interests.   All societies regard loyalty to one's own society as right and betrayal as wrong.   All societies value social stability and cohesion, and all condemn the activities of social delinquents with penalties for transgressors. Although property may be communally or individually owned to varying extents, there is also a universal concept of theft.   All societies find it necessary to have rules to ensure that their individual members behave towards each other with a measure of respect.   All these rules are often broken, of course, but they are still there.

It is also important to look *behind* the differences. For example free, universal systems of formal education in the modern sense did not appear until the nineteenth century.   But this does not mean that there was no such thing as a right to be educated until the nineteenth century.   For it was still true even in prehistory that the young needed to be *trained* in how to hunt, fish, sew, cook, light fires and so on.   They still had to be 'educated', albeit primitively, for the benefit of the tribe and for themselves *as* members of the tribe.   So there *has* always been a right to be educated in one way or another; it is not a modern invention.

We seem to have (a) a core of universal, basic norms to be found in all societies, this core being at the basis in each case of (b) a more variable 'superstructure' of conventions, customs and ethical interpretations which differ from culture to culture and from one historical period to another. So we do not have *variances* from one society to another, we have *variations* around a set of *norms*. This suggests a modified form of relativism which could perhaps be called 'structural relativism'.

In this sense one of the most cogent examples of relativism is that the rights of the individual are emphasized in the West but not to the same extent in the East. This difference is for complex historical and cultural reasons which would take a separate book to summarize. East and West both recognize the validity of individual rights and the necessity for authority in society, but the bias is different in either case. The West gives special emphasis to the rights of the individual, whilst in the East there is greater respect for tradition, authority, duty and the ethic of the social group. Each, therefore, will have a different concept of rights.

Also, consider the "core moral precept" which we identified as a necessary condition for any society to function. It is as non-specific, of course, as the truism that 'human beings must eat in order to live', a statement which, though true, does not tell us *what* human beings should eat or how food should be cooked. There can be different *interpretations* which will vary from one culture or society to another and from one era to another. Further, although the core moral precept is universal it is often 'hijacked' and sometimes ingeniously modified by this or that ideology, belief system, political creed or social pressure group which hardly helps clear thinking, let alone anything else. Human conflict is often unavoidable too, with rights and wrongs on both sides, complicated even further by the 'tribe over the hill mentality' where human beings behave ethically towards each other within their own *group* but very differently towards outsiders.   But none of these considerations invalidate the core moral precept itself.   It is still there.

'Relativism' as a thesis needs to be formulated with some care.   It is correct to say that some things are relative, but to say that 'everything is relative' leads to absurdity.   Specifically, the sentence 'everything is relative' must, if true, be relative *itself*, so it is incoherent and self-refuting. Aristotle made much the same point over two thousand years ago when he pointed out that saying 'there is no such thing as truth' is only to contradict yourself.   Perhaps the most infantile argument for relativism is to say that Einstein's Theories of Relativity prove that relativism is true.   The fallacy here, of course, is that Einstein was writing about space and time.   He was not writing about ethics, human societies or customs or about "human rights".

Or again, suppose an internationalist or multi-culturalist were to argue that different systems of rights and of ethics are 'equally valid'.   This sounds tolerant, open-minded and so on, but taken literally this would confer validity by default on totalitarian systems as under Nazism or Stalinism. If we are told, oh no, that sort of thing isn't valid at all, then where does this leave the original assertion that different systems of rights and of ethics are equally valid? The answer to the puzzle, of course, is given through *structural relativism* as explained above.

Which Rights are Absolute? Human rights theory makes a distinction between '*prima facie* rights' and 'absolute rights' (sometimes called 'inalienable rights'). This is a distinction which political and mass media rhetoric fails to make, and this failure is productive of much misunderstanding about rights. Also, an *important* right (such as free speech) does not necessarily mean that it always takes precedence over other considerations.

A *prima facie* right is based upon clear moral obligations by others. To contravene, deny or ignore such a right constitutes *infringement*, *violation* or *abuse* - under normal circumstances. Obvious examples can be given - the rights to freedom, to free speech, the right to life, the right not to be killed, the right to privacy and many of the other rights which we have encountered in this book.

However - such rights can, in the most exceptional circumstances, be modified, forfeited or sometimes annulled altogether, and throughout this book we have seen examples of how this can happen for valid and overriding reasons. You have an important *prima facie* right to freedom, but if you are a serial killer you will, in most civilized countries, forfeit your right to freedom for a considerable time, maybe for life. We have explained in some detail how your right to free speech has valid exceptions, how your right to privacy can be validly interrupted, and how even your right to be told the truth can have valid limitations. Another example: you have a *prima facie* right to be respected, but you will forfeit this right if you do something contemptible, e.g. child abuse.

'Absolute' rights are also based upon clear moral obligations by others. But these differ from *prima facie* rights in that they can *never* be validly altered, denied, annulled, ignored or contravened in *any* circumstances. The most obvious examples include your rights *not* to be defrauded, robbed, attacked, raped, murdered, enslaved, persecuted or discriminated against. No circumstances can ever justify these actions.

Recalling the definitions given in Chapter One of *negative rights*, *positive rights*, *claim-rights* and *liberty rights*, 'absolute' rights are *negative claim-rights* that other people should not do certain things, without exception. By contrast, *prima facie* rights consist mainly of *liberty rights* and *freedoms*, which are always conditional, and *positive claim-rights* which, as we have often seen, can have limitations. This explains the difference between *prima facie* rights and 'absolute' rights.

Perhaps the most basic 'absolute' right is the right to *justice*. This right can be held by anyone in any circumstances whatsoever - even a convicted war criminal, for example, still has a right to justice. It is beyond the scope of this short book to give a full exposition of justice but the reader will recall, from Chapter Two, its linkage with the universalizability of moral rules with the all-important corollary that it is *wrong* to treat people arbitrarily. As we said, this is a *necessary condition* for justice, implying *inter alia* the necessity for *consistency*. But justice does not mean 'even Stevens' equality or equality of outcome, as we explained in Chapter Five. Rather more intricately, it means *the determination of morally valid equivalences, differences or differentials by relevant and consistent criteria.* This applies to 'distributive' justice (pay, reward, benefits etc.) as well as to 'commutative' justice (determination of appropriate sanctions or penalties for an offence, as in a court of law).

How Real are Rights? *Reductionism* is a spectre that sometimes haunts human rights theory. This is the thesis that rights terminology is semantically superfluous in the sense that any sentence referring to 'a right' or 'rights' can be rephrased *without loss of meaning* in a moral terminology that does not require reference to 'rights' at all. Does it mean, therefore, that 'rights' are unreal?

First, though, consider some examples. We commented in Chapter Three that 'we can say perfectly clearly that it is wrong to neglect the life-critical needs of others whether we talk in terms of *rights* or not'. In fact the first paragraph of Chapter Three said a number of important things about the life-critical needs of human beings without referring to rights *once.* Likewise, consider major examples of human rights abuse such as war crimes, mass murder, mass deportations, slave labour, the routine use of torture, imprisonment without trial, suppression of dissent, and so on. The fact that these are major moral wrongs and extremely serious crimes can be stated quite clearly without using the terminology of rights. It is superfluous in that it does not add anything to what has already been said, or to what is already known. Arguably, it is unecessary to say that mass murder (for example) is an abuse of rights when we already know that it is a major moral atrocity.

Reductionism means *equivalence of meaning*, not 'no meaning'. To say that people have a right to be told the truth is no different from saying that (other) people are obliged to be truthful to their fellow human beings. To say that you have a right to freedom is the same as saying that other people should not unwarrantably interfere with you. To say that you have rights not to be attacked by others means that other people have moral obligations not to attack you. And so on.

Reductionism occurs in other senses too. In Chapter One we noted that when we talk of 'having rights', this does not mean that rights are 'things' which are 'part of what we are'. The word 'rights' does not in any literal sense denote intangible *things* which we walk around with. 'Rights' is a *relational* term, about 'freedoms, claims and entitlements arising out of the personal, social, moral, legal and political *relationships* between human beings', and we have spent a considerable proportion of this book explaining in detail the various relational concepts which comprise 'rights'. These are, of course, the claims, liberties, permissions, powers, prerogatives, immunities and their various combinations which we looked at. But they are not 'parts of us' as individuals, or attributes which we 'have'. Comparably, A and B are physical objects, but the distance between them, AB, is not another physical object, nor is it an attribute of either A or B, for *distance* is a relational concept. Of course, distance is not 'unreal', and so it is with rights. Reductionists do not say that rights are unreal, simply that they are relational concepts, not *things*.

Also, we noted in Chapter Two that rights terminology only began to appear in early mediaeval times. Prior to that, Plato, Aristotle, Confucius, Christ, Mohammed, Buddha and many other great thinkers and teachers had a lot to say about what was good or bad, just or unjust, but their failure to mention 'rights' can hardly be described as an *oversight*. They were, after all, very intelligent people. The history of human ideas is a very scholarly and fascinating topic, but we will merely note that 'rights' first came to be used in civic, legal and political contexts to denote *relational parameters* between human beings regarding powers and entitlements. The interesting question is whether rights terminology was *invented*, or did it *evolve*? We suggest the latter, but we can say with some confidence that if rights are 'natural' things or attributes which all human beings possess in the same literal way as they have bodies or minds (or needs, wants, desires etc.), their existence would have been noticed and commented on long before mediaeval times.

We also noted in Chapter Two that although the Christian Bible says a lot about what is good or bad, right or wrong, there is no mention within it of 'rights', either 'natural rights' or 'human rights'. However, we also recorded that 'the American

Declaration of Independence asserted that 'all men.....are endowed by their Creator with certain inalienable rights...'. How can this be, in view of the fact that the Bible does not mention 'rights'? The American Declaration of Independence was, of course, a political document, not a philosophical thesis on the basis of rights. In terms of what was literally said (or rather, not said) in the Bible, we could perhaps say that the Founding Fathers simply got things wrong (plain wrong, in fact) when they wrote their Declaration.

A more charitable interpretation given by some human rights theorists is that although the Bible did not mention rights *as such*, the concept of a right was *implicit* in what it said about how people should or should not behave. Thus 'thou shalt not steal', for example, implies - or suggests - a moral right that things should not be stolen from you. But we do not quibble with this interpretation, in fact we welcome it. For it bears out what we have been saying within this book: that rights are based upon ethics in the first place and that 'rights are *constructs* out of ethical concepts, or *derivatives* from them' (Chapter Two).

The remaining question is whether ethical concepts and/or rights concepts derive from a transcendent God. This raises the curious question of whether something is 'good' because God ordains it or whether God ordains it because it is good. But we leave that question to the theologians. For the purposes of this book, we will merely reiterate that the basic ethical principle of respecting the interests and concerns of others is a necessary condition for any society to function and this, we suggest, is true whether God ordains it or not. It could be suggested that this is the way God planned it, but here again, let us not digress into theology.

The important thing is that *reductionism* does not deny rights any more than sub-atomic physics denies the existence of molecules. It is not a spectre at all, really. All we have to do is to remember that rights are not *things* which are 'part of what we are', but *relational concepts*. They are still perfectly real.

Seven - Conclusion

For many people, 'rights are rights' and they are fundamental. This is the message that comes across from politicians and the media, and there is, of course, an important kernel of truth in this. But as we have seen, there are different *types* of rights which have important differences. Some are clear and unequivocal whilst others are contingent, sometimes tenuous, and uncertain. There can be non-rights as well as rights, and many rights are conditional upon other people's obligations which can sometimes be limited by circumstances or resources beyond their control, as distinct from culpable default. Even quite important rights, such as the right to medical care, can be less certain than 'absolutist' human rights rhetoric might lead us to expect.

Likewise *freedom* has a vital role in human affairs but it is, nevertheless, limited by various qualifications and conditions for perfectly valid reasons. It does not mean 'anything goes' or being 'free' of valid legal or moral constraints. This is merely adolescent - or dictatorial - debasing and derogating the importance of other people's freedoms. The right to *equality* is highly complex and often ambiguous. Passing laws on equality quotas etc. do not alter the basic issues involved for moral and procedural equality do not necessarily entail material equality.

It is also a common confusion to equate rights with needs, interests, aspirations, wants, wishes or desires. It is true that rights are often *about* needs, interests, aspirations and so on, often very important ones, but the relationship is much more complex than *entailment* pure and simple.   Otherwise I could say, 'I need a cigarette, therefore I have a right to a cigarette'.   You do not have to be a logician or a moral philosopher to see that this sentence is a non-sequitur, and the same applies to any other sentence or argument of that format *unless further reasoning is provided.*   People who think and talk primarily in terms of rights are advised to remember this.

We also noted that *having a right* and *the right thing to do* can be very different things.   Failure to understand this can lead to wrongs against other people, sometimes serious ones.   Thus we have an answer to the question we posed in the Introduction - you *can* be 'within your rights' but also 'in the wrong' over something, without logical or moral incongruity.   In many situations one right can validly take precedence over another according to circumstances, *moral perspective* and the *comparative harm* principle.   Otherwise we end up with permanent 'rights deadlock' between my rights, your rights, his rights, her rights and everybody else's rights, taking us on a wild goose chase forever and ever from one person's rights to another's.   This is why 'rights' cannot be the fundamental moral concepts as some theorists suggest.   People who think and talk primarily in terms of rights are advised to remember this.

Human rights *abuse* comes in two forms: *hard* abuse and *soft* abuse.   Hard abuse has clear, vivid examples: war crimes, mass murder, mass deportations, slave labour, the routine use of torture, imprisonment without trial, suppression of dissent, and so on.   These are major moral *wrongs*, extremely serious crimes which, when they are known about, invite universal outrage and condemnation.

Soft abuse of rights is very different from hard abuse.   Whilst hard abuse denies rights for invalid reasons, soft abuse over-emphasizes rights.   In Chapter Two we mentioned *Rights Talk - The Impoverishment of Political Discourse* (1991) by Mary Ann Glendon.   She relates how modern Americans over-emphasize rights and are prone to discuss moral, social and political issues in terms of the rights of A *versus* the rights of B.   This tends to promote conflict rather than to resolve it, as well as creating a culture of excessive individualism. She criticizes rights talk for its *silence* on the entire question of responsibility, shifting the moral emphasis from the individual as a moral agent with responsibilities to a 'rights holder' who makes claims and demands.   Many present-day citizens of the UK will find that much of what she says sounds very familiar.

Maybe Jeremy Bentham was right all along when he criticized 'natural rights' as 'dangerous nonsense'.   Rights can also be misperceived by the naive, the immature, the irresponsible and their apologists as a spurious 'moral shield' against criticism, condemnation and/or punishment.   The language of rights lends itself very readily to self-justification and to excuse-mongering, and it is important that rights are not perceived as a wrongdoers' charter.   Human rights legislation which leaves itself open to such an interpretation could end up, in the long term, by making the law look silly and making rights look silly.

We should also mention *rights hypocrisy* and its cousin, *moral myopia*. A classic example occurred in 2006 when a Danish magazine published a cartoon satirizing Mohammed. During the ensuing fuss a French journalist appeared on television giving an eloquent defence of the magazine using the standard, almost 'off-the-shelf' arguments - fundamental, basic freedoms of expression and of publication etc. etc.. But it seemed to be overlooked that Moslems also have rights, such as the rights not to be offended or insulted.

Another phenomenon is 'third party' rights over-emphasis where an individual, organization, government or legal system is so concerned with the rights of some special group that this is to the detriment of others. For example it is very commendable that a paediatrician should be primarily concerned with children's rights, but it is *not* alright to overlook the rights of parents not to be falsely accused of serious crimes against their own children.

The unavoidable conclusion of this book is that 'rights' is a very cogent and useful terminology to use in various contexts (moral, legal etc.), providing its ambiguities and complexities are properly understood. It focuses moral attention upon the interests and concerns of individuals which majoritarian or utilitarian considerations might sometimes overlook. But its over-use results in *dogmatization* which glosses over complex issues where majorities and other individuals have rights too.   It also leads to rights over-emphasis which, as with the inflation of a currency, only debases and diminishes its value.   People who think and talk primarily in terms of rights are advised to remember this.

Further Reading

Conquest, Robert. - *The Great Terror*. Macmillan, 1968.

Dembour, Marie-Benedicte. - *Who Believes in Human Rights?* Cambridge University Press, 2006.

Dworkin, Ronald. - *Taking Rights Seriously*. Harvard University Press, 1977.

Edmundson, W.A. - *An Introduction to Rights*. Cambridge University Press, 2004.

Feinberg, Joel. - *Social Philosophy*. Prentice Hall, 1973.

Flew, Anthony. - *'Social Justice' Isn't Any Kind of Justice*. - Philosophical Notes No.27. Libertarian Alliance, 1993.

Freeman, Michael. - *Human Rights*. Polity Press, 2002.

Glendon, Mary Ann. - *Rights Talk: The Impoverishment of Political Discourse*. Free Press, 1991.

Glover, Jonathan. - *Causing Death and Saving Lives*. Penguin Books, 1977.

Hare, R.M. - *Moral Thinking*. Oxford University Press, 1981.

Hart, H.L.A. - *Are There Any Natural Rights?* Philosophical Review 44, 1955.
- *The Concept of Law.* Oxford University Press, 1961.

Hohfeld, Wesley Newcomb. - *Fundamental Legal Conceptions.* Yale University Press, 1923.

Levy, Neil. - *Moral Relativism - A Short Introduction.* Oneworld Publications, 2002.

Melden, A.I. - *Rights and Right Conduct.* Basil Blackwell, 1959.

Solzhenitsyn, Alexander. - *The Gulag Archipelago.* Harper & Row, 1973-78.

Thomson, Judith Jarvis. - *The Realm of Rights.* Harvard University Press, 1990.

Wallace, Jonathan. - *Natural Rights Don't Exist.* The Ethical Spectacle, April 2000.

Index

abortion - 90
abuse of rights - 119
aid (foreign) - 46
altruism - 36
Alzheimer's Disease - 49
American Declaration of Independence – 26, 116
anarchism, anarchy - 61
apartheid - 24
Aristotle – 25, 72, 110, 115

Bentham, Jeremy – 26, 120
Burke, Edmund - 26
Buddha - 115

Capone, Al - 100
Charity Commission - 33
Christ - 115
claims - 53
claim-rights – 17, 53, 67
competition - 37
complex rights - 68
Confucius - 115
crime and punishment - 97

DNA - 91
discrimination - 74
divorce - 40
Dworkin, Ronald - 21

Einstein - 110